# THE HIDDEN HOUSE

## Jenny Robertson

**Scripture Union**
130 City Road, London EC1V 2NJ

© Jenny Robertson 1987
First published 1987

Other *Tiger Books* by Jenny Robertson
*The Beggar Girl and the Prince*
*Seal Songs*

**Acknowledgement**
**The author would like to thank Mrs Sheila Webb and**
**Mrs Edith Easton for patient help and advice, also**
**the Scottish Spina Bifida Association for literature**
**and information, but also, most especially, Ann**
**Atherton and Susie Easton just for being themselves.**

ISBN 0 86201 434 4

Phototypeset by Input Typesetting Ltd.,
London SW19 8DR
Printed and bound in Great Britain by
Cox and Wyman Ltd., Reading

# Contents

# 1

## New neighbours

'Our new neighbours will be arriving tomorrow,' said Mrs Brown. 'How would you two boys like to give me a hand? I want to give the house a last tidy up for them.'

Callum Brown and his friend Paul looked up from their game.

'Do we have to?' Callum asked his mother.

'Someone's got to,' she replied.

'Come on then.' Paul flipped a miniature football into its tin.

'I'm just putting on my boots.' Callum's voice jerked with the tug and pull of each foot.

'That's the trouble with being a home help,' Jean Brown said as she opened the gate into the next door garden. 'I'm never done with cleaning.'

The sunset shone into the glass of the front door. Rooks flapped across the glen.

'It's nearly Christmas,' Callum said.

'Christmas. Aye. I'm getting a computer,' said Paul for the thousandth time.

A computer. And Paul's nine year old sisters, Susan and Claire were getting snazzy roller skates. Someone else at school was getting an amazing bike . . . but Christmas, the real Christmas, was like buried treasure, hidden away underneath torn wrapping paper and too much dinner, thought Callum. His thoughts were interrupted by Paul.

'Do you know who your new neighbours will be?'

'A family with a girl about your age,' Mrs Brown

replied. 'The dad is working abroad, it seems.'

The setting sun shone into the empty front rooms.

'Oh dear, look at all those cardboard cartons. They should never have been left here. And there are still ashes in the fireplace.'

'It feels spooky!' Paul said. 'Did old Mrs Mack die here?'

'No, she was taken off to hospital as soon as she became ill,' Mrs Brown answered briskly. 'And even if she had died here, what difference would that make? So suppose you take those cartons out to the bin?'

'Okay.'

Callum sat on the floor with his sticks beside him and stacked boxes together.

'I'll carry them out, Cal,' said Paul, sliding a box over his head.

'Beep-beep-beep. Computer Pelican programmed for action.'

Callum tried it too. 'Can't see . . . where I'm going.'

Boxes crashed to the floor.

'Programme's failed. Re-run for action.'

'How do we open the back door, Mum?'

'Now, sober up, boys. You're not being much help. Here!' Jean Brown brandished a long-handled key. 'Out you go. Squash the boxes flat and you'll get them all into the bin. Then, Paul, perhaps you could carry the bin down to the gate.'

'All computers wrecked.' Paul jumped up and down on a pile of boxes. 'Disaster day dialysed.'

'Dialysed's to do with kidneys, dumbo. At least, dialysis is.'

'Okay, you're the medical expert.'

Beyond the yard the frosty hill glowed in the last of the light.

Callum listened for deer. Instead, he heard owls hoot from the forest.

'Stay away from my Place, owls,' he thought.

But he didn't tell Paul. Callum's Place was a secret.

Paul trundled the bin to the back gate. Callum went too.

'Come on, Cal. We'd better go and help your mum.'

Mrs Brown was cleaning out the fireplace. 'Just give the mantelpiece a dust, please Callum, and, Paul, would you take those ashes out? If there's still room in the bin, that is.'

'Yes there's still some space left. I hope the new people are grateful for all your hard work,' said Paul.

'Housework's the sort of thing you only notice when it isn't done. Watch that pan, Paul. If you shoogle it there'll be a right mess on the floor.'

'There's plenty of dust here,' Callum coughed.

'Shake the duster outside. Then you can both go home.'

As Paul set off for his home, Ballonoch Farm, a car pulled up. It was Callum's father, Jim Brown, the local vet.

'Hi there, Callum! Is that you going out or coming in?'

'Both really. Mum's cleaning up next door.'

'I'll make her a cup of tea. Where are you off to?'

'Just out the back.'

'Don't be long. It's getting dark.'

Callum nodded and set off as quickly as he could, which was never as quickly as he wished. Jim Brown watched his eleven year old son manoeuvre his sticks across the drive. Then he turned into the house. Callum heard the front door shut as he paused for breath. The only other thing to be heard was burn water. Callum headed over a wide flat path, blowing smoke signals with his breath.

Once upon a time six or seven small stone houses stood between Callum's house and the burn.

'Arches of roses,' Mrs Mack, his old neighbour, always used to say, 'and who knows what before that? But there was always the laughter of bairns at play.'

Now the houses were nothing more than scattered

7

stones. Not a wall remained. All that was left, just where the path came to an end, was a stone chimney with a square bare hearth. That's where Callum headed for. It was his Place.

He lowered himself on to a stone beside the ruined hearth and laid his sticks on the ground.

'I hate it when things change,' he thought.

Of course there were changes all the time in the Place: windy days or sunshine; rowans with blossom or berries. Or bare and dead – like now.

But nothing was really dead. Not even Mrs Mack, little and thin like a sparrow. Well, yes, she was dead because her body had died. . . . Callum wished he had someone he could talk to about Mrs Mack. Not Paul, who was scared of ghosts. Not his mother. She could only drive cobwebby thoughts away. There was always his dad.

'He understood about the baby blackbird,' Callum recalled.

He opened his hand, remembering the feel of the featherless fledgling which fell out of its nest the day Mrs Mack died.

Tulips and sunshine, birds singing everywhere, and this little body stiff in his hand. Then his Dad's voice, quoting: 'Not one sparrow falls to the ground without your Father's consent.'

'But it's a *blackbird*, Dad,' Callum objected.

He buried the fledgling here in the Place.

His thoughts whirled back to the present.

'I've missed *Sportsround* . . . I'm starving.'

But he still had things to think through. Those new neighbours would take over Mrs Mack's house. There wouldn't be anything of her left, and she'd been Callum's special friend.

There was a lonely feeling inside him. He took a last long look round his Place, and as he set off home he came across the fawn.

It was lying right in his path.

'Oh!' Callum stood as still as he could.

'Parp!' barked the adult deer from the forest up the hill. The fawn lifted its head. It had a creamy fleck just behind its attentive, delicate ears.

'It must have strayed down to the road looking for food,' thought Callum. 'It's been hit by a car.'

He took another step closer. The young animal bounded to its feet at once and leapt almost out of sight. Almost, but not quite. In the last of the light Callum saw the fawn topple back down on the frozen ground, Callum hurried down the path, stumbling and righting himself again with his sticks.

'Dad, come quick! There's a fawn up the hill. It's hurt.'

'But it's dinner time. I'm just dishing the potatoes,' Mrs Brown objected. 'Your dad was up most of last night,' she went on, 'and he's had to work today, even though it's Saturday.'

But Callum begged, 'Please, Dad, come and have a look. I know you say deer aren't easy to treat, but. . . .'

'But this one's different? How far away is it?' Dr Brown asked.

'Not far. It couldn't run, you see.'

'What do you think, Jean?'

'Oh dear, I know you two!' Mrs Brown sighed. 'Well, go on then, and don't complain if your dinner's ruined!'

'Of course not, Mum!'

What were burnt potatoes compared with an injured fawn?

'Why were you called out, Dad?'

'Calves always choose unsocial hours to be born.'

'Look, Dad, there's the fawn. It's got wind of us. It's going into the woods. It must have a family waiting for it.'

'The forest is the best place. Deer belong to the wild. They're vulnerable creatures, you know.'

'What's that mean?'

'Easily hurt,' his father explained as they stood staring

at the empty hillside and the dark outline of the woods. 'They're hard to help, you know, Callum. They give up too easily. But when your fawn could run like that I'd say it should mend okay. I think we'd better go home.'

'Couldn't we have left some milk for it, Dad?' Callum asked as they ate their reheated dinner.

'That could have done more harm than good. I'm not sure what strength would be safe for a fawn. Cow's milk isn't always the best thing.'

'I'll go out first thing in the morning and see if there's any sign of the deer,' Callum said.

But next morning there was no sign of the fawn. Callum stood on firm, flat, ground, listening.

'Is that you, deer, barking up in the woods? You're telling me the fawn's all right. It's better for you in the hills than shut away in the zoo,' he thought.

It would have been nice to have been able to have tamed the fawn and kept it as a pet. But that's the sort of thing which happens in films or stories.

'Real life's different,' Callum told himself firmly.

Real life meant he had to wear boots with metal supports to help him walk because before he was born bone and nerves in his spine hadn't formed in the usual way. Real life meant that he couldn't climb the rough hillsides or do things as fast as other boys. But he just got on and did things as best as he could anyway. Real life meant that old friends died and new people came to live next door. Real life meant that fawns got injured because they were hungry, but ran away without getting any help because they were afraid of humans.

The church bell rang from the village, warning Callum he'd better hurry.

'Come on, Callum,' his mother called from the car.

Callum climbed into the back.

'So the fawn's well away?' his father asked. 'Let's hope he mends. We'll keep a watch out. The wintry weather may bring the deer back from the hill.'

# 2

## *Julie*

'Do we *have* to move house?' Julie demanded.

'Oh, Julie, I've told you a million times already. It's the best thing. I'm doing it for your sake really.'

'But I don't want to leave Tracey, Dawn and Rachel.'

'I know, dear, but you'll soon make new friends. It's such a nice little school you'll be going to. It will do us both good to live in the country.'

'You promised we wouldn't move again.' Julie was near to tears. 'I'm not going!'

'Please don't be difficult, Julie.'

'I'm not going,' Julie repeated. 'I like it here. Why can't Dad work at home?'

'Because he's got a good job in Yaristan. . . .' But Julie had rushed upstairs.

We moved here when Dad got his job. Now she's making me move again. It's not fair, she thought, staring at her half packed things.

At tea-time Mrs Murray tried to cheer Julie up. 'You'll love our new house, Julie. And there are sure to be children around.'

'I don't care,' said Julie. 'I don't want to leave my friends.'

'Perhaps we can have them to stay.'

'You said that the last time, and Sarah was the only one who came. I don't even see her now. It's never the same when you move.'

'No, but Julie, do try to look at it from my point of view. I feel I need to make a fresh start. Listen, love, since we're going to live in the country, I'm sure I can do what I've always promised.'

'What's that?'

'Buy you a dog.'

'Oh, Mum, would you really?' Julie leapt to her feet and turned a cartwheel. 'What sort shall we get?'

'Now, hold on, Julie. Let's get into our new house first. Then we'll see what's available.'

'I hope it's a lab, a honey labrador puppy, like we saw at that farm last year.'

'We'll see. And now I must get on. I've got so much to do. Have you packed those boxed games yet? And what about the doll from Uncle Bruce?'

But Julie was already away on the telephone. 'Tracey, is that you? Oh, hi! Yes, it's Julie. Guess what! We're going to get a puppy!'

Julie got presents from Tracey, Dawn and Rachel. Her whole class sent cards like, 'On the move', 'We'll never forget you', 'The cows and sheep don't know what's coming to them'. There were loads of Christmas cards too. It all added to the last minute packing.

'I feel like a pop star,' she said, as she got into the car. 'But it's all right for them. They're staying here. I've got to go right away where I don't know anybody and start all over again.'

But her mother only sighed and changed the subject.

'We mustn't get too far ahead of the removal van. It will be a slow journey, especially on the hills.'

It was. Julie fell asleep. She woke up in time to see a rainbow across wide still water.

'There you are, Julie,' said her mother. 'That's specially to welcome us. There's just been a heavy shower and now there's a rainbow.'

But the rainbow didn't cheer Julie up.

'Are we there yet?'

'Another thirty miles.'

'Thirty miles!'

'Oh, come on, Julie, that's not far. It's just that the removal van is slow.'

'When can we go and look for puppies?'

'Soon, Julie. Give us a chance to settle in. Tell you what, why don't you watch out for signs which say, "Puppies for sale"?'

So Julie did, but she didn't notice any signs until they passed a farm on the very last bend of all.

'Look, Mum, it says "Ballonoch Farm. Puppies for sale. . . " ' she began, but her mother was already saying, 'There's our new house, Julie.'

'Oh, where?'

They pulled off the road, up a side lane and into a driveway. A hill rose behind them. Open country stretched ahead. There was one other house close by and nothing else in sight.

Mrs Murray switched off the engine. 'Here we are, Julie. Journey's end.'

At that moment Mrs Brown appeared at her gate.

'Welcome to Ballonoch. Would you like a cup of tea? You must be tired after your long journey.'

'That's very kind of you, but the removal men should be arriving any moment.'

'Well, suppose I bring the tea across to your house? The men will probably be glad of a cup. Do let me know if there's anything you need.'

'Who's that?' Julie asked.

'Our new neighbour. She seems nice, doesn't she?'

'Has she got any children?'

'I don't know. Come on, let's have a look round the house. I'm sure you're going to like it. Look, there's an open fireplace.'

'What does that mean?'

'You burn coal there. Or wood. But there's central heating as well. Come and see your bedroom. It's up in the loft. It's all been specially done up for you. Do you think you'll like sleeping under that sloping ceiling?'

'It's all so bare and empty.'

'It won't be, once we've got carpets down and furniture in. There's the van coming now.'

The doorbell rang. It was Mrs Brown with tea and scones.

The doorbell went again.

'That'll be the electricity man,' said Mrs Murray again.

But it wasn't. It was a boy on sticks.

'That's our son, Callum.'

Julie stared. A boy! Did he have any sisters? What a stupid name! Callum. And why did he wear those metal things round his legs?

'Come and say hullo, Julie. How nice! A friend for you.'

The doorbell went again. This time five removal men crowded into the kitchen along with the electricity man who turned on their meter.

'I'll go and top up the teapot,' Jean Brown disappeared and Callum went with her.

'You'll be glad of this tea,' said Julie's mother to the removal men. 'It's been a long journey, hasn't it?'

'Long enough, but no' the worst we've done. A few weeks back one of our vans blew right off the road.'

The men swapped stories of moves and journeys. Mrs Murray poured out more tea. Julie stared out of the window. But there was nothing outside except hills, fields and trees.

'I hate it here,' she told herself.

The kitchen reeked of tobacco smoke. But the men were already stubbing out their cigarettes.

'We'll go and unload. Carpets first, eh?'

After that the house began to fill with furniture.

'It's funny seeing our things in a different place, isn't it, Julie?'

'Some place! I'm never going to like it here, Mum. There's nothing to do. And that boy isn't going to be a friend at all. He's got a stupid name.'

'Callum?'

'That's it. And he wears those boots with metal rings round his legs.'

'Calipers. Yes, I noticed that as well. Poor boy. He can't help it. You sound as if it's his fault, Julie. His mother seems very nice.'

'Armchair in this room?'

'Yes, please, beside the fire.'

'Tea chest?'

'That's for the loft. Can you manage? The stairs are rather steep. And very narrow. Go on up, Julie. You'll be able to start organising some of your things. And, look, there's your bed.'

Julie followed her mattress up the steep narrow stairs. Nothing felt right. Her felt tip pens and drawing books, her personal stereo and tapes, her jewellery and dressing table set looked at her from the top of the tea chest. They didn't feel like hers any more.

'They don't like this bedroom either,' she thought.

Yet if she'd read about this loft room in a story she would have loved it, she knew. The winter sun streamed through sloping windows. She could see for miles . . . only there was nothing to see.

Fields. And cows.

'Stupid cows!'

One coughed and she jumped.

She looked out over the hill at the back.

'I could take my puppy for walks up that hill.'

But the removal men interrupted that day dream. 'Does this dressing table belong up here?'

'Yes, that one's mine.'

A bundle of bedding followed. 'Hope there's not much more for up here. The stair's that narrow.'

'Did you manage all right?' Mrs Murray called from the bottom step.

'Just. We were beginning to think we'd have to take it through the window.'

'My neighbour's just making a fresh pot of tea.'

'That's fine. We could be doing with a break.'

They went downstairs. Julie turned back to the window.

A small figure stumbled across a flat path along the foot of the hill. It was the boy next door. Where could he be going? Julie pushed the window opened and leant out. She could hear the sound of water. A rough barking sort of sound came from the woods further up the hill. The boy Callum stopped and looked in its direction. Then he set off again towards the burn.

It's all right for him. He's lived here all his life. He belongs. I never belong anywhere, thought Julie bitterly.

What was he doing now? He sat down in the middle of nowhere. Well, there was a heap of stones. Stones. That's all that there was here. Stones at the front. Stones at the back. Nothing but stones.

Julie shut the window.

I wonder who lived here before, she thought.

The house was about a hundred and fifty years old, her mother had said. Maybe there would be a ghost.

'Julie, would you like a cup of tea?' Valerie Murray called.

Tea, in that cigarette atmosphere with unpacked boxes everywhere, the men's talk, and her mother and the new neighbour making friends – no thanks!

I hate moving house, thought Julie, staring at the darkening sky. And that's when she saw the deer. A mother and a fawn, picking their way across the side of the hill, leaving the safety of the woods. For food, maybe. Julie pushed her window open with a sound so slight she didn't notice it. But the deer did. With one bound they were away, the mother in front, the fawn following. They stood still for a moment on the crest of the hill, and then disappeared into the wood.

Julie rushed into the kitchen.

'Mum, there's deer on the hill. They're hungry. Have we a saucer of milk or something?'

'I don't know if deer drink milk, Julie. But you're right about them being hungry. A fawn got injured yesterday. Mrs Brown was telling me. Callum found it. You can hear the story when you go in for your meal.'

Callum noticed the deer too as he rearranged fir cones in the fireplace. He couldn't tell if the fawn was the same one as he had found, but he decided that it probably was.

'I'll go to the farm tomorrow. Paul's dad might let us have some hay, he thought. Oh, they've disappeared.

He eased his calipers under him. I don't think I like that new girl, he thought for the hundredth time. She's not very friendly.

'She's probably upset at leaving her friends,' his mother had said as they went back home to refill the teapot for the removal men.'

'Did you see the way she stared at me?'

'No, I didn't notice anything.'

But his mother sounded uneasy and Callum said, '*You're* staring now, Mum. Don't look so upset. I tell you one thing. I think Mrs Mack will be feeling sad about it.'

'What a lot of nonsense! Mrs Mack's beyond all that now. . . . I must do some potatoes, and we'll ask our new neighbours in for a hot dinner. That new lady seems very nice. But she doesn't seem very organised.'

'Give her a chance!' Dr Brown came into the kitchen with an armful of logs.

'I'll sort some of these out for the folk next door.'

'Do you think dead people know what's going on down here?' Callum asked.

'What a thing to worry about!' his mother said as she refilled the teapot. 'Mrs Mack had a long, happy life,' she went on. 'She trusted God for everything. The only thing which made her sad was that both her children emigrated.'

Callum nodded. 'People have to go,' the old lady told him once. He remembered the conversation because it had made him start thinking about the Place. 'Think of the big changes since I was a wee girl in the houses beside the burn,' Mrs Mack had said. 'There's nothing but a rickle of stones there now.'

'There's a fireplace,' Callum said. 'I've noticed it standing all on its own. Did you live there once then, Mrs Mack?'

Next time he went up the path towards the burn he stopped to look more closely at the fireplace.

I wonder if that was Mrs Mack's chimney? Perhaps her family lived in this house when she was young.

From then on, Callum made the fireplace into his den. The path made it easy enough for him to get there. He didn't tell anyone else. Not even Paul, who wasn't interested in old houses or stones. And now he certainly wasn't going to let Julie know anything about his Place. 'She's not that sort of person either, he thought as his mother called him in for tea.

# 3

## Hidden treasure

*My secret Place is beside a burn. It's a place where*
*dreams don't come true, but they might.*
*Children played here sixty years ago. And roses grew*
*here. Mrs Mack said so. Animals shelter here.*
*Sometimes you hear deer. You can hear larch trees*
*sing. I buried a fledgling here. Mrs Mack said there*
*might be treasure hidden here.*

'My goodness, listen to this!'

Julie and her mother were sitting beside Mrs Brown's
fire. Valerie Murray was skimming through a book and
a torn, handwritten page fell out. She picked it up and
read it aloud.

'That's just something Callum's written,' said his
mother from the table.

'But it's beautiful . . . Mrs Mack is the old lady whose
house we now have, isn't she?'

'Callum was very fond of her.'

'He seems an imaginative boy, don't you think so,
Julie?'

But Julie's thoughts leapt to the glimpse of Callum
she'd seen from her window as he'd headed towards the
burn and sat amongst old boulders. So that's his den,
she thought. His secret. Aloud she said, 'Some secret!
It's just a load of old stones!'

'What's that, Julie? Well, Jean, this is most kind of
you. Are you sure there's nothing I can do to help?'

'Not at all. Jim's just cutting the joint. And here's
Callum. Goodness, what a scruff! Away and wash your

hands.'

But Callum was staring at the piece of paper his mother's visitor still held between her hands.

'That's mine!'

'I thought it must be. It's wonderful, Callum. . . . Why, what's the matter, dear? It was lying inside this book about old stones. Julie and I must find out more about our new neighbourhood. It seems fascinating. . . .'

'Callum, will you please go and wash your hands.'

Without another word Callum turned on his sticks and went out to the kitchen.

'Oh dear, this is most distressing!' Mrs Murray stood up and went to the kitchen door. 'I'm sorry, Callum. I never guessed this was something private.'

'Of course it wasn't, Valerie. Don't upset yourself. Callum shouldn't leave things lying around. Now, everyone, let's all sit down. You must be starving, Valerie, driving all the way, and then the unpacking.'

'Your scones and tea kept me going. What a good baker you are!'

'That's kind of you to say so. Come on, Jim, will you give thanks?'

So they sat round the table and Dr Brown prayed aloud, 'Heavenly Father, thank you for bringing Valerie and Julie here. We pray that you will bless them in their new home. Thank you for providing for all our needs.'

'Amen,' Callum and his mother said, and 'Thank you, that was kind,' said Mrs Murray politely.

The grown-ups found plenty to talk about. Callum and Julie sat and ate in silence, though Julie brightened up when her mother said, 'Julie and I are going to buy a puppy as soon as we've settled.'

'A puppy? Oh!' said Mrs Brown.

Callum knew exactly the thoughts behind his mother's words. Dog dirt on the lawn, constant barking, her husband called in repeatedly for help and advice. . . . Luckily Dr Brown was more positive.

'That sounds like a good idea,' he said with a smile at Julie. 'We'd have one ourselves, but you know what they say about cobbler's children. . . .'

'Always the worst shod! Don't tell me it's the same for vet's pets! I shouldn't think you would have much time for puppy training, Jim. We'll bear that in mind when we get ours.'

'Now, now, that wasn't meant to be a hint. We've had a few pets ourselves, haven't we, Callum?'

'What kind of pets have you had, Callum?' Valerie Murray was doing her best to be pleasant.

'Hamsters,' he managed to tell her.

'Very nice.'

'*Mum*, you hate hamsters. You never let me have one!'

'Well, I must say I'm not very fond of rodents. But I'm sure hamsters are very sweet. How many did you have, Callum?'

'Three.'

'All at once?'

'No.' He was behaving badly, he knew, but he couldn't help it.

After the meal, in the process of tidying up dishes and sitting back beside the fire for coffee, Julie hissed, 'It's only a heap of old stones!'

'How do you know?'

'That would be telling!'

'Pass the biscuits, Callum. Are you sure you won't have any, Valerie? Oh, of course you must get back to your unpacking. Jim's got some logs for your fire. And, Julie, will you be starting our village school?'

'We thought we would wait till after Christmas.'

'Yes, the term's almost over. I'm sure Julie will soon make plenty of new friends,' said Jean Brown reassuringly.

She's going the right way about it, Callum thought.

'She'll be starting secondary in August, won't she? his mother went on. 'It'll be nice for her to know a few children before she goes to the big school.' And Callum noticed his parents exchanging looks.

They think I won't cope with changing classrooms all the time, he thought, but I play football and everything.

Of course he'd never make a school team, like Paul, but he played goal in friendly matches in his wheelchair, and he'd saved quite a few goals too, some of them tricky ones.

Amidst goodbyes and thank yous Julie and her mother went back home. As soon as they'd gone, Callum picked up the crumpled paper and threw it in the fire.

'That girl must have spied on me!'

'You weren't very friendly,' his father said.

Callum stared at the flames which licked his secret. Some secret!

'Mrs Murray said she was sorry about your poem.'

'She was only being polite.'

'Callum, Mrs Murray didn't mean to offend you.'

But above the crackle of the fire Callum's silence said that he thought she had been nosey.

'Listen, son.'

He nodded, staring at the flames.

'Sick animals . . . that fawn you wanted to help. . . . People can be hurt as well.'

'I know.'

Of course he knew.

Jean Brown bustled in from next door. 'Poor souls! It will be ages before they're straight. I should think Mr Murray is pleased to be away abroad, far from all that muddle.'

The phone went.

'That'll be Auntie Helen. She always phones about this time on a Sunday. Unless it's a call for you, Jim. Hope not . . . 5760. Hullo. Oh, it's you, Helen. Have you got your Christmas pudding boiled yet? What's that? Yes, we're fine. . . .' Mrs Brown moved the telephone through into the kitchen and shut the door with her foot as she talked.

Callum poked the fire. The log hissed and gave off a

spicy smell. 'It must be larch,' he said.

'It is, but it has to burn before it can give off that good smell. Why not burn your bitter feelings too?'

'About Julie, do you mean?' Callum said aloud. To himself he thought, she called the Place a load of stones. I won't tell her anything about it now. That's for definite.' Aloud he said, 'I'm going to ask Paul's dad for a bale of hay.'

'For the deer?'

'Aye. I'll go to Paul's straight from school tomorrow.'

'Okay . . . now, tell me something. What do you think Mrs Mack meant about hidden treasure?'

'She said there's a story around about silver.'

'You don't think she was getting muddled up? There have been plenty of finds in this area, including that old bell we saw in the museum in Edinburgh, do you remember?'

'I think so, but it was a long time ago. It came from Kilmichael, just down the road.'

'Callum, is that you still sitting there? Off you go!'

'You've got no boots on, son, have you? I'll give you a hand to the stairs.'

As his father helped him along he said, 'Why not call for Julie after school and take her along to the farm with you?'

'I don't think Paul would like it.'

'Come off it, Callum, that's just an excuse.'

But as Callum shuffled upstairs on his bottom he knew he didn't want to do what his dad asked. Not yet.

He went into the bathroom on sticks he kept upstairs.

Mrs Mack knew a lot, he thought as he undid the extra zips his mother sewed in his trouser legs and unstrapped the bag he needed to wear because of his paralysed bladder. If Mrs Mack said there was hidden treasure lying around she might easily be right.

The trouble was he couldn't leave the path to go and look.

He went into the bedroom, sat on the floor, pulled off

his socks and examined his feet in front of a low mirror. Sometimes his socks chafed him. Or his bootlaces were pulled too tight and because he had no feeling he had to look carefully to see if there were any sores.

But we must get the hay organised first, he thought as he crawled into bed.

He sat up in bed and tried to pray as usual. But he still felt sore about Julie.

I know Julie is hurt in some way, he thought. But I don't want to take her to the farm for the hay. Just the same, Dad's right. I should try to help her. Making a big effort, Callum managed to pray, 'I'm sorry for feeling bad about Julie. Help me to be nicer to her.

He felt better now. Not the farm, he decided again. Paul won't like it. But there will be some other way.

His mother put her head round the door. 'Did you manage the bathroom all right? How about your feet? Let's have a look, in case you missed anything. . . . Oh, dear, what cold feet,' she rubbed them between her hands. 'Night night'.

'Night night.' He turned off his light.

Next door, under the eaves, Julie cried herself to sleep.

# 4

## A loose stone

'Callum didn't like it when you read his poem, did he?' said Julie to her mother over breakfast.

'I'd no idea he'd get so upset. He seems a very sensitive boy.'

'What does that mean?'

'Full of feeling.'

'I hate him!' declared Julie.

'Now, Julie, don't be like that! Just think what fun we're going to have in this new house.'

'There's only cows and fields here.'

'Oh dear, look at the time! Perhaps I'd better try to light the fire?'

'What do you have to do?'

'Find a match. Where did that big matchbox go? This is hopeless! We're never going to find anything.'

'Can we buy our puppy today, Mum?'

'Oh, Julie, I've got a hundred and one things to do.'

'You promised.'

'Yes. I know I did but not today. There's loads of unpacking still to be done. And we'll need to go off in the car to Fynestown – that small town we drove through. I must buy some food. Oh dear, this fire doesn't want to light.'

'Tracey's big brother put paraffin on their bonfire last Guy Fawkes' night.'

'That was very dangerous surely? Blow hard, Julie, there's a spark here that looks as though it might go up in flame.'

'It's all black and the coal's fallen down where the paper burnt.'

'My granny used to hold a sheet of paper in front of her fire to get it to catch. There, see how the fire is sucking the paper in.'

Mrs Murray tugged the paper away. The flames which had burnt brightly behind it died down but they could tell that the fire was going to stay lit.

'What a job! Most mornings I'll turn on the electric one.'

'Dad will help you when he comes home. Why can't he come home more often? It's not fair!'

'I've told you before. He's got a good job out there. He'll be home next year some time, for a holiday.'

'Next year! That's ages away. I want Dad to come home now. Then we can go back to our old house. I'm never going to like living here.' Julie raced up to the loft and flung herself on her unmade bed.

I've lived in six different houses and loads of hotels: half as many houses as years of my life. I hate moving all the time and losing my friends, she thought.

The doorbell went.

'It's no one I want to see,' Julie told herself. 'In our old house it would have been Tracey or Dawn calling for me. It's only Mrs Brown.'

'Julie,' her mother called, 'are you dressed yet?'

Julie didn't answer. She heard voices. The front door shut. Then her mother came upstairs. 'Hurry up, Julie. Jean has to go into Fynestown too. We can come with her, she said, and while we two are in the shops you've got a special invitation.

'Where to?'

'Jim phoned to say if you wanted you could go round to his surgery. Someone's just brought a kitten in. He thought you might like to see it. He's going to take us out in his car on his next day off, down to the sea and all over the place.'

'The sea?'

'It's only six miles away. . . . So hurry up, Julie. I know settling in isn't easy, dear, but I'm sure you're going to like it in the end. We're lucky to have such kind neighbours.'

'*You* are, you mean.'

'Listen, Julie, you mustn't judge Callum just because he can't walk properly. Hurry up and get dressed. I wonder where I put my purse. I said we'd be out in five minutes. I'll never be ready.'

Julie didn't mean to be slow, but she couldn't find any of the clothes she wanted to wear. It was another fifteen minutes before she was ready, but Mrs Brown said she quite understood. Once in the car the two mothers chatted above the noise of the engine, while Julie, alone in the back, stared out of the window. A humpy hill stuck up on her right.

'If Jim were here he'd be telling you all about our history. That's Dunadd. It was a very important place once. The first kings of Scotland were crowned there.'

'How interesting! We'll have to go and have a look sometime, won't we, Julie?'

'I'd rather go to the farm where the puppies are.'

'Perhaps we'll have time for that later today. . . . So you know Bruce McIntyre quite well, Jean? He's actually promised to get me a job.'

'Did he now?' Jean Brown glanced in the driving mirror at Julie, who stared carefully out of the window. 'Be careful, Valerie,' she said in a low voice, which Julie just overheard, 'Bruce McIntyre . . . oh, I'm sorry, I shouldn't blacken him, especially when he's a friend of yours.'

'He was a colleague of my husband actually.'

But Julie saw the back of her mother's neck redden.

She doesn't want to tell the truth, she thought. He bought me that doll. A doll for someone of my age! But Mum said it was very expensive. She told me to make sure that we packed it.

'Here we are now.'

'Thank you, Jean, it's so kind of you to give us a lift. Come along, Julie,' her mother said in the polite kind of voice she used over the phone. 'This is going to be a real treat for you. I'm sure you'll enjoy seeing the animals.'

I don't have much choice, Julie thought as Dr Brown came out to meet them.

While the two mothers went off to shop, Julie stayed at the surgery.

'Cup of coffee, Julie? Or juice? Ah, here's Peggy, our receptionist.'

Peggy had long red nails and a friendly smile. 'Hi, there, Julie,' she said.

After that time flew by. When Mrs Murray reappeared Julie held out ten crimson finger nails and a book called, 'How to take care of your dog'.

She told her mother all about her morning as they ate yoghurts and cheese rolls at lunch.

'Dr Brown's nice. He said he'd take me out on his rounds sometime with Callum. So long as it's not in the middle of the night.'

'No, I should think not. Poor soul! I wonder if he gets called out often.'

'I think he does. He's got another vet working with him so they share night work. And there was the cutest wee kitten. She'd hurt her claws. And there was a collie. Dr Brown wouldn't let me touch it, though. Mum, you should have seen it! It got caught up in some machinery and its side was all in a mess.'

'Poor thing!'

'Mum, you're not listening!'

'Yes, I am. It's very interesting. I told you that you would like it here. . . .'

'Peggy's nail varnish is lovely. I wish I had long nails like her. Mum, couldn't we go to Ballonoch Farm this afternoon to see if there are any puppies?'

'Oh, Julie, how you go on! All right then, but I'm not letting a puppy over the threshold until we've got properly unpacked. What a nice fire this is! I'm sure we'll soon get used to lighting it.'

'I like it too,' said Julie, holding her red nails out to the flames. 'I like the way the flames lick the coal. It's friendly.'

And above the hiss and chatter of the fire Julie said, 'Mum, you didn't come here just so that you could marry Bruce, did you?'

'Oh, Julie, what nonsense!' said her mother's lips. But her face said something different. Julie jumped up and ran outside. She's going to marry Bruce. I know she is. I'll never see Dad again. I wish I could run away.

But there was nowhere to go to. Cows stared at her. Julie felt a bit scared and so instead of going across the field, as she first thought, she headed towards Callum's Place.

'It *is* just a lot of old stones. I don't believe a word that Callum wrote about hidden treasure.

Just the same, she put out her hand and touched one of the fallen boulders. Once it had been built into a wall. It had been part of someone's house.

The wind blew Julie's hair across her mouth.

There's nothing here now, and there's nothing for me either.

But she decided to explore. She wandered around the stones until she came to an old fireplace, filled not with wood or coal or flame, but with fir cones.

Callum must have put them there.

And now she was sorry she had laughed at him. She knelt in front of the hearth and fingered the scattered cones. Some were very small; others were large and spikey.

From where she knelt she could see the sky sailing out of the chimney, like smoke in a child's drawing. She pressed herself into the chimney. Loose stones scrabbled beneath her.

I'm the fire burning up the chimney.

But it wasn't a very wide chimney and she felt

squashed. She wriggled out again, chipping her red nails. As she pushed herself back into the fir cone hearth, one of the stones inside the chimney moved. Loose chips fell about her. A bit warily, because she didn't want Callum to know she'd been here, Julie pushed at the loose stone. As she did so she felt something wobble underneath her hand. The stones fitted together so neatly that, by dislodging one, Julie had moved another deep inside the wall.

It should be all right, though, she told herself. But Callum's right to choose this place. It's a place which says, 'Come and see'. I wish I'd found it myself.

She touched the moss at the foot of the wall. I'd like to make a garden and plant flowers here. But it would be hard work digging up the thistles.

From her vantage point she could see her mother come into their back garden. 'Julie, Ju-lie!'

Julie decided not to shout back. She'd invaded Callum's place and the least she could do was not bring a grown-up here. She ran back as fast as she could.

'Hi, Mum!'

'Where have you been?'

'Across there, beside the burn.'

'Don't run off without telling me where you're going. Suppose you'd fallen and broken your leg? I wouldn't know where to look for you. But you were upset, weren't you? Was it about Bruce?'

Julie nodded, but instead of explaining about Bruce and Dad or finding out all the things that were worrying Julie, Mrs Murray said quickly, 'Listen, dear, I noticed Christmas trees in the shops. We'll go back to Fynestown tomorrow and buy one, shall we?'

Christmas! She'd almost forgotten about Christmas.

'Dad hasn't sent my present yet, has he?'

'The posts might be slower here. Look at all those fir trees! It seems silly to buy a Christmas tree when they grow all over the place . . . but we'll get one just the same. Well, how about a walk along to the farm to see if they have any puppies?'

'Oh, *yes*! Shall we take the car?'

'Nonsense. It's only along the road. You'll have to get used to going for walks if we get a dog.'

'Not if, when. Going for walks will be fun with a dog.'

Sheep bleated from the fields. A car swished by.

'This *is* a beautiful place,' Mrs Murray said. 'I know you'll be happy once the first new feeling has gone.'

'Perhaps,' said Julie, testing a thickly-iced puddle and watching it splinter. 'It's funny, Mum. In town there would be lights and decorations.'

'Yes, Christmas trees in every window and all the shops packed to the doors.'

'There's a Christmas tree shining in the window in the farm. But I suppose farmers work at Christmas just like other days.'

'You're right, Julie. Animals have to be looked after whether it's a holiday or not. Those holly bushes know it's Christmas, anyway. Just look at all those berries! What lovely decorations they would make!'

But soon Julie forgot about Christmas decorations. There were five labrador pups in one of the farmer's sheds: two honey ones, two brown and black ones, and one, the smallest of all, was jet black. . . .

'. . . and absolutely gorgeous. Oh, Mum, can't we have this one? Oh, please, Mum, it would be the best Christmas present ever. Can't I take him home with me?'

But Mrs Laidlaw, the farmer's wife, shook her head.

'I'm sorry, dear, but they're all spoken for. We breed them, you see, and we only mate the dogs when we can be fairly certain of finding buyers. But there might be some more pups in three or four months if you're interested.'

'I think we can safely say "yes" to that, unless we find one somewhere else first,' said Mrs Murray. 'Don't be too disappointed, Julie.'

'My twins love this black puppy too. Would you like to stay and play with him, Julie, while I give your mum a cup of tea? Then you can get some juice when the twins come.'

For an enchanting fifteen minutes Julie stayed in the shed with the puppies and pretended they were all hers. Especially the black one. She held him close. His eager tongue licked her face and hands.

'I love you. I'd call you Jet. There you are! How do you like that name, you jet black darling?'

She put Jet on the uneven floor and he trotted to her feet and tugged at her shoelaces.

'Come on then,' she picked him up and hugged him again as two girls ran into the shed.

'You've got Blackie' said one.

'Are you Julie?' asked the other.

Julie looked from one to the other. Blackie! Jet was a much grander name.

'We're Susan and Claire,' said one of the twins.

'You've to come in for your juice,' said the other.

One twin was a bit taller than the other, but they looked exactly alike. Their voices were identical too.

'Can your mother tell you apart?'

'Of course!'

'Not many other people can.'

'Do you always dress alike?'

They nodded. 'Sometimes we choose different colours.'

'I think twins should be allowed to dress differently if they want to,' said one of them.

'But we'd probably end up choosing the same thing,' said the other, and they both laughed.

'Your mum's waiting.'

Julie fondled Jet. 'Goodbye,' she whispered.

As they went into the farm Julie said, 'Your mother says she's going to have some more puppies soon.'

'Our mother can't have puppies,' giggled the twins, and Julie saw the funny side as well. Their mothers looked round as the three girls burst into the kitchen giggling and choked into their juice.

'Do come round for a cup of tea some time,' invited Julie's mother. 'In fact, why not make it Boxing Day? I'll invite Jim and Jean and Callum too. We can have a little housewarming, though you'll have to excuse the mess I'll be in.'

'Come to our Nativity Play first,' begged the twins.

'We're angels,' said one.

'When is it?' asked Mrs Bates.

'On Christmas Day. It's a Sunday School play.'

'Jean Brown runs the Sunday School. I'm sure Julie would be very welcome there.'

Julie didn't say that she thought Sunday Schools were boring. Just then Paul put his head round the door.

'Mum, can Callum have a bale of hay?'

'I should think so.'

'Thanks!' And Paul was off again.

'Come along, Julie. We really must go.'

The twins are nice, but they're too young and they giggle too much, thought Julie as they said goodbye.

On their way home they passed Paul pushing Callum and a bale of hay in Callum's wheelchair. Callum was trying to balance the hay on top of him as well as hold his sticks.

'You're getting into a mess,' observed Mrs Murray and Julie giggled. 'They look like Worzel Gummidge,' she said, knowing they couldn't say anything back with her mother there.

As they walked on Julie looked back at Callum, wedged in his chair beneath the hay. He doesn't know I've been to his Place, she thought. I wonder what he would say if he knew?

# 5

## Waiting for a secret

Julie watched Paul and Callum trundle their hay round the back of the house.

I wish I had disco boots. They'd go well on the drive, she thought as the boys parked the wheelchair beside the gate into the field.

'There's that girl watching us,' said Paul. 'She's too full of herself.'

'Aye, she is a bit,' Callum agreed. 'Where will we put the hay?'

'On the fence. We can stick the posts through it.'

But the bale was too thick to wedge on top of the fence.

'We'll have to climb over,' Paul said, so Callum clambered over the gate.

That's not bad for someone with sticks, Julie thought as Paul bundled the bale of hay over.

Julie climbed up on their gate. She kept her back turned to the boys who were spreading hay over the edge of the field. Instead she looked at Callum's Place. I've never seen Paul go there, she thought. It's just something for Callum and me.

Callum and me! But they were barely on speaking terms.

The boys turned towards the gate. Julie ignored them, and Paul ignored her. 'Do you want us to open the gate?' he asked Callum, just as if Julie weren't sitting there. 'It will save you climbing over.'

'The catch is too stiff. We'll climb over as usual.'

Without looking, Julie could tell Callum was having a struggle to get over the gate with her sitting there too. He needed to heave himself up with his arms and roll over the top.

'Get out of the way, can't you?' said Paul.

'No.'

'Callum can't get over.'

'Tough.'

'Aye, that's what I'll need to be,' threatened Paul. 'Get off before I shove you.'

'No.'

'I'm slipping!' Callum slid down the gate and Paul started to push Julie, but she clung on hard.

'Get off!'

'No. Ow! Stop shoving me!'

'Cal needs space!' Paul said through his teeth.

He shook Julie. The gate rattled and Julie wobbled.

'I'm not getting off for either of you!' She tried to push Paul off, but she lost her balance and fell.

'Come on now, Cal,' said Paul, but before the boys could get on to the gate Julie scrabbled up to the top again.

Paul kicked out at her. Julie grabbed his legs.

'No one ever fought here before you came,' Callum said and Paul added, 'So go away. We don't want you.'

'I don't want you either. I didn't want to come here.' She gave one more tug at Paul's flailing feet and turned away. But where could she go to? Not back home just yet, not across fields where cows might chase her, not along unknown roads in the winter dusk.

'Julie, wait! Julie!'

That was Callum. He struggled over the gate and Julie paused, looking back. Callum's Place glowed in the frosty sun.

'Julie, I'm sorry. You're new. We shouldn't have tried to push you off like that,' Callum called. He hobbled towards Julie, but she ran on.

She heard his feet slither over small stones. He

stopped, balancing on his sticks. 'Julie, I'm trying to say sorry if you'll only listen.'

But she wouldn't stop. He's trying to be nice but I don't care. He belongs. I haven't got anyone.

She searched the edge of the forest and hid behind a thick fallen tree. She heard Paul and Callum push the wheelchair away, heard her mother call her, but she didn't move.

She didn't think about me when she made me move here, she thought as she stumbled over bumpy ground beside the singing burn back towards the ruined houses where other children had lived and played once; back towards Callum's Place.

I'm going to knock that old fireplace down. I'll stamp on all the fir cones. Then Callum won't have his Place any more. It's only a load of old stones anyway.

It was almost dark. Owls hooted. Julie felt scared. Her hands were cold. She trampled the fir cones easily, but although she thumped and pulled and pushed, the stones in the chimney remained intact.

All except that one wobbly stone. She could waggle it like a loose tooth. And just like when you wobble a tooth and feel the roots tear, Julie felt something give in the middle of the chimney. A shower of loose stones fell around her feet.

'Julie! Where are you? Julie!'

That was her mother. Then Dr Brown's voice called, 'Julie!'

Torches flashed on the hill.

Julie gave the stone one more tug and dislodged moss and small broken stones. It looked a bit messy now, and the stone in the middle seemed very loose. Perhaps Callum would think the cows had bumped into it.

'Ju-lie!'

They mustn't find her here! She ran back the way she'd come, falling, hardly able to see. She jumped on to the road, almost in front of a car.

No wonder deer get hurt! Julie watched its tail lights

disappear. The road seemed empty and silent once it had gone. A lamp wobbled out of the dark. It was Callum. He had a bike lamp clipped to his belt. 'Everyone's looking for you: Dad, Mum, your mum and me.'

She felt bad, but she wasn't going to say so.

'They'll drive the deer away. They won't come out of the woods with so many people about, and then they won't find the hay.'

'Oh!' was all Julie could say. Callum blew a whistle and she jumped.

'What's that for?'

'To tell them I've found you. Come on.'

The lamplight lurched as he walked. She slowed to his pace.

'Does it hurt?' she asked suddenly.

'What?'

'To walk?'

'The calipers are heavy.'

'Yes, I s'pose they must be. Have you always been like that?'

He nodded, 'It just means I can't get around as much as I'd like.'

'I know.'

Or get over gates, he might have said. Sorry, he had said. Paul hadn't said sorry. But she had started it. And now she'd have to face his parents and her mother with no real reason why she'd run away.

'She's here!' Callum yelled.

'That was very naughty, Julie,' her mother scolded. 'Look at the inconvenience that you've caused, going off on your own in the dark.'

'It was my fault too,' Callum said, generously.

But it hadn't been Callum's fault at all. Paul's perhaps, not his. And now his fir cones were trampled and his Place was a mess. He won't ever want to be friends with me when he finds out, thought Julie.

'Well, now we can all go in for our dinners,' Jean Brown said. 'It's good to see you safe and sound, Julie.

Your mother was worried sick.'

Julie felt herself blushing.

'The golden rule is never go off without telling anyone, and especially not at night,' said Dr Brown as the grown-ups said, 'Good night' and 'Thank you' and 'Not at all.'

'We're going to dress our Christmas tree this evening,' Mrs Brown told Julie. 'Would you like to come round later and help? We set up a crib as well.'

'All right,' Julie said.

'You mean, thank you very much,' her mother corrected her, ushering her home to eat sausages and potatoes beside the crackling fire.

'We'll buy our tree tomorrow, Julie,' she promised, switching the television on.

Julie stared at the fire. Does she care about me or doesn't she? Will she marry Bruce or stay with Dad?

She didn't like to ask.

'Will you buy me disco boots for Christmas?' she said instead.

That evening she helped Mrs Brown and Callum dress their tree. She arranged wooden animals around their crib. She looked at a dog book with Callum. She went into Fynestown again with her mother next day and chose a Christmas tree.

'But I don't feel Christmassy without Dad,' she said.

'Why ever not? He's been away most Christmasses. Have you ever thought what that must have been like for me?'

No, she hadn't thought.

She bought six silver fir cones and two wooden bells.

'Are they for the Christmas tree?'

'Perhaps'.

I'll put the fir cones in the Place, and I'll tidy up the mess while Callum's still at school.

On her way across to the Place with the fir cones and the bells, Julie was pleased to see that animals had obviously eaten Callum's hay. She hoped it was the deer. And now Julie had a splendid idea.

Instead of the new fir cones, which her mother would expect to see on their tree, she would put hay in the fireplace, just like Callum's Christmas crib.

In fact why not make a crib?

I've got toy animals somewhere, she thought, and I might even find an angel or a baby doll.

Fired with her idea she raced across to the Place, cleaned away the trampled fir cones and did her best to brush away the fallen stones. She tested the wobbly stone. It was very loose, but it was still in place. Deeper in the chimney, she knew, another stone had been dislodged but she didn't think Callum would notice.

She hung her bells on a small stone which jutted out above the hearth. Then she ran back up to her room and found her old toys.

There was a costume doll with a feathered hat. He would do for Joseph. She lifted a pretty mother doll from Africa who had a baby in a bundle on her back.

'They'll do for Mary and the baby Jesus.'

She wondered if she should tell her mother what her to-ings and fro-ings were about. But it would give Callum's secret away. Now she had a secret too, a Christmas secret.

'I'm just going over towards the burn,' she called.

'What, again?'

'I like it there,' Julie said.

Carefully she arranged her stable scene right inside the fireplace beneath the wooden bells.

She sat back on her heels, pleased. There were voices from the road. That would be schoolchildren coming home. Callum usually got a lift. Susan and Claire had invited her to the farm. It was Christmas Eve. Suppose Callum didn't go to his Place till after Christmas Day?

But he'd certainly go and check the hay.

Julie made a tracking sign with smooth pebbles and pieces of hay. She put it at the gate, pointing to the Place. Then she ran home and washed her hands.

'The twins have invited me to the farm.'

'Don't be too long. Remember we've still to dress our tree.'

'Okay, Mum.'

'You seem happier today.'

Julie turned to give her mum a wave. 'Perhaps she's lonely too,' she thought as she set off to find her new friends and see Jet.

'His new owner is coming this evening,' said Susan, or perhaps it was Claire.

'He'll be someone's Christmas present,' Claire, or perhaps it was Susan, explained.

'Wish he was ours!' they chorused.

'Me too!' Julie agreed.


Julie was right about Callum and the hay. As soon as Callum got home he dumped his bag in the kitchen, gulped the drink his mother always left for him, snatched a biscuit and hurried outside to see if deer had touched the bale of hay.

He noticed the tracking sign and guessed at once that Julie had put it there.

She must have been to the Place while I was at school, he thought. The Place was on everybody's map, it seemed. Perhaps Julie had even brought her mother there.

He went on slowly, feeling sad.

And then he saw the stable scene.

Julie's done that for me, he guessed.

It was funny to think someone else had been in his Place.

What was it Mrs Mack had once said: 'Places are for people.' And then she had opened her Bible. 'My eyes aren't as good as they used to be. Can you read this?' Her knotted fingers pointed to the page and Callum read aloud, 'I will give you treasures from dark, secret places and you will know that I am the Lord.'

Callum always thought those words had something to do with the Place. But his Place wasn't secret any more, not now Julie had put her Bethlehem stable there.

Now the Place belonged to Julie every bit as much as it had belonged to him. Callum sat down beside the fireplace and fingered the dolls and animals, the little black baby wrapped in African cloth lying on real hay.

I hope the cows don't come, he thought.

But Paul had said the other day that his father was keeping the cows in the lower field till after Christmas.

And just at that moment Julie arrived. She held a silver star in her hands.

'It's for the stable.'

'Did you put your crib in the fireplace?'

'Do you mind? That I've been here, I mean.'

'Not too much. I've been thinking. This Place is meant to be shared.'

'Do you really think so?' Julie's face lit up. 'I'm glad you don't mind about the stable. It's a kind of Christmas present.'

'It's a good present. In fact it's one of the nicest things that have happened in the Place for ages.'

She squatted beside him and re-arranged the stable scene.

'The Place has come alive now.'

'It was never completely dead. Just waiting.'

'What for?'

He hesitated. 'Waiting for us. And waiting for a secret.'

'What sort of secret?'

'I'm not sure. Mrs Mack knew.'

'You mean the hidden treasure you wrote about?'

'Aye . . . maybe. Mrs Mack showed me something about it in the Bible.'

'About the Place? What did she say?'

He closed his eyes and concentrated. 'I will give you treasures from dark secret places and you will know that I am the Lord.'

'The Place isn't dark, at least not very dark, but it is a secret, isn't it, Callum?' There, she'd said his name.

'You're lucky to have found it.'

'It doesn't belong to me at all. I'm glad you found it for yourself.'

'I wouldn't have found it on my own. But I saw you from my window the day we arrived. Then Mum read your poem and made you mad.'

'Yes, because I thought it was my secret. But I was wrong.'

And now Julie wished she could tell him she'd been wrong as well, far more wrong than Callum. He'd only wanted to keep his Place a secret but she'd tried to knock it down. But she didn't say anything and now it was getting dark. Christmas stars pricked the sky.

'It's really Christmassy now even if there aren't any fairy lights or tinsel,' said Julie. 'Let's hang my silver star up, shall we?'

Callum hung it from a jutting out stone above the bells.

'I've never felt so Christmassy in my life,' Julie went on, 'but it's a quiet Christmas feeling.'

'As quiet as the stars?'

She nodded. 'Do you think it's really true about Jesus in a manger?'

'Yes, I'm sure it's true.'

'I think I am tonight as well. For the very first time.'

'Let's say a Christmas prayer.'

She folded her hands as a teacher had shown them once at school. 'I don't say prayers much, except to ask God to bring my dad back home, but Dad hasn't even sent me a present,' she added, unfolding her hands.

'Oh, Julie, I'm sorry. And you've given me such a special Christmas present.'

'God hasn't made your legs better either, has he?'

'No, he's not a magician. He gives us presents though, like the stars in the sky.'

'And the Place,'

'And Jesus in the hay.'

'The toy Jesus, you mean?'

'Yes, and the real Jesus. Let's say our prayer.'

'All right.'

So Callum prayed, 'Thank you for us being friends. Thank you for Julie's stable and the animals and everything. Please help Julie to be happy here and may her dad know she's missing him. Amen.'

'Amen,' said Julie. 'That was a good prayer, Callum, but I think 'Amen's' a silly word. Ah ! men! Why not Ah! women!?'

'It's just the way prayers have to end,' said Callum.

'I think we should say "Love from Julie and Callum".'

'I've never said that at the end of a prayer.'

'Well, next time we say a prayer I'll say the words at the end.'

'All right. Say them now, if you like.'

So Julie folded her hands again and said, 'Dear God, can you hear me? I'm saying love from Julie and Callum, lots and lots of love because we're friends.'

Then they turned away from the Place. They stopped for one look back. The stable scene hardly showed against the dark stones. Callum stumbled, but Julie caught hold of him. Then they heard a tearing sound.

'Shsh!' they both said, 'it's the deer.'

'It's a mother and baby,' whispered Julie.

They stood very still while the mother deer munched the hay.

A car swished by on the road. The deer took fright and bounded away.

'Look, Julie, the fawn's got a white mark on its head. Did you see it?'

'No, it's too dark and it ran away too fast.'

But Callum was certain he'd seen it. 'It was the fawn I found.'

'The one that was hurt? So it must be better now. That's good,' and as Julie ran into her house she thought, 'This is going to be the very best Christmas ever.'

Her mother looked up with a smile, 'There's been a last delivery of mail, Julie.'

'Oh! Is there. . . .'

'There's a card from Great Aunt Vera. Open it carefully. She usually puts money inside. And, look, Julie, there's a parcel for you.'

'From Dad!'

And now she knew for sure this was going to be the very best Christmas ever.

# 6

## Christmas

When Julie opened her eyes next morning she found a bulging stocking at the end of her bed. She took it downstairs and climbed into her mother's bed to open it. Then Mrs Murray gave Julie her present – a heavy package with red disco boots. Julie had bought jewellery for her mother who put the painted glass beads on over her dressing gown and went to get their breakfast.

'Did Dad give you anything?' asked Julie.

'He sent a cheque. Open your parcel while I put the kettle on.'

Julie's parcel had come from an expensive London store. Her father must have ordered it by post, so it wasn't his fault that it wasn't quite the right size for Julie, or that it didn't suit her new life running over the fields behind Callum's Place.

It was a party dress with layers of petticoats and lace. It was flecked and flowery and full.

'It must have cost a fortune!' Valerie Murray exclaimed. 'Try it on, Julie. It's a model dress, the sort of thing children from the very richest families wear when they go to parties. In a few years' time you'll give anything to have a dress like that!'

'But I don't go to parties, and it's a bit too big.'

'Too big is better than too small. You'll grow.'

Julie hardly recognised herself in the mirror. 'I don't look like me,' she said, 'I suppose Dad has forgotten what I look like.'

'Wear your lovely dress today, Julie. We're going to

church, remember, and out to the hotel for our lunch. Jean invited us to share their Christmas dinner, but I didn't want to intrude on their family meal. I know you and Callum don't get on too well. . . .'

'We do now, Mum. I'd much rather go there than to a hotel.'

'It's all arranged now. The Browns have invited us for tea, so you'll see them later. I'm looking forward to going out for a meal. It will be a treat for me; and what a beautifully dressed daughter I'll be taking too.'

'The twins will wonder what's happened when they see me all dressed up like this.'

But the twins were too excited about being angels to notice Julie's dress. Callum did though. 'You look different.'

'It's from Dad, from an expensive London shop.'

'I've never been to London . . . I'm glad his parcel came.'

'I got disco boots too. Are the crib people all right?'

'Our Place is looking great.'

*Our* Place. Julie felt a glow go through her. 'You've been then?' He nodded, but then they had to stop talking because the service was beginning.

During the prayers Julie glanced at Callum's bowed head. 'He really believes it all,' she thought. 'It's not just something he's doing because we're in church.' She tried to concentrate, but the prayers were so different from the way they had prayed in the Place. Still, the play was good, except the twins felt self-conscious and got a fit of giggles.

After the service people stayed to talk. Callum's parents introduced Valerie Murray to other grown-ups. Callum and Paul chased around, with another boy, jerking Callum's sticks, like guns, having a mock fight. He's a bit childish when he's with other boys, Julie thought, feeling a bit left out, but then the twins came up.

'Happy Christmas,' they chorused with a lot of giggles.

'We got disco boots,' Claire, or was it Susan, said.

'Oh good, we can skate up and down together.'

'Come on now, Julie, it's time to go off for lunch.'

'Happy Christmas, Julie. I believe you're coming this evening? We'll look forward to that.'

'Happy Christmas!' Julie greeted Dr Brown. 'How's the kitten?'

'Safely home for Christmas.'

'What a pretty dress!' Mrs Brown said.

'It's from my dad,' Julie explained. 'It came with the very last post yesterday.'

'From Encore,' Valerie Murray named a smart London store.

'My goodness. . . . Well, we'll see you both later. I'm looking forward to a chance to have a chat, Valerie.'

As they crossed the road to the hotel Mrs Murray said, 'You'll be the most expensively dressed person here, Julie. Walk tall.'

I'd rather be wearing dungarees and disco boots, Julie thought.

The hotel was full and the other people all seemed to know each other. There were plenty of jokes from one table to another, but no one talked to Julie or her mother. There were long pauses between each course and Julie felt bored.

I wish we'd gone to Callum's, she thought.

'Why don't you have a walk round and look at those doggy paintings?' suggested Mrs Murray, and she might have done, just for something to do, but then her mother added, 'Everyone will see your Christmas dress.'

'I'd rather just stay here.'

'Well, sit up straight then, and stop playing with the cutlery.'

Julie was glad when the long meal ended. 'Please can we go home? I want to try my disco boots before it gets dark.'

'And I shall put my feet up! All right, Julie, let's go.'

But Julie could tell that her mother didn't want to

leave the dining room and all the chatter, even though they weren't part of it.

They paid their bill and got into the car.

'I wonder if the hills know it's Christmas Day,' said Julie.

'No fairy lights here!' her mother started the engine.

'Perhaps that's right. There wouldn't have been any in the stable, nothing but animals and hay.'

'And angels, remember. . . . I hope we made the right decision after all in coming here. It *is* very cut off.'

'Oh, Mum, do you mean we can move back home?'

'How can we do that, Julie? This is home now. Why don't you try your new disco boots while there's still some daylight?'

'I might. I'll have to change out of this dress though.' So Julie changed into her dungarees and put on her disco boots. The countryside was empty apart from her. She glided along on high red wheels, feeling tall and adventurous. Her easy pace and her heavy boots made her think of Callum who could only walk when his legs were cased in metal.

But he never seemed to mind. Instead he looked after hungry deer and knew about exciting things like buried treasure.

And now it was time to go to Callum's for tea. As she left the darkening world, Julie turned to look at the countryside around her which still waited to be explored. When I get my dog, she thought, but that seemed further away than ever.

They ate their tea around the fire; and afterwards Callum, Julie and Dr Brown played games while the mothers talked and Christmas music played from the Browns' music centre.

Next day, sprawled out in front of the fire, Julie wrote thank you letters.

'Is that letter for Dad? May I read it?' her mother asked.

*Dear Dad,*

*Thank you for the dress. I wore it to church and to the hotel where Mum and I went for lunch. It's beautiful. I hope you had a nice Christmas. I've made friends with the boy next door. His name is Callum. At first I didn't want to come here, but I like it now, only I wish you would come home.*

*Mum says she needed a new start and Bruce is helping her get a job. I wish you could get a job here. I miss you very much. Have a Happy New Year.*

*Lots of Love,*
*Julie.*

'I don't think you should have written that about Bruce and the job.'

'Why not? It's true, isn't it?'

'Yes, but . . . oh, you're probably too young to understand.'

'I'm not too young to have to say goodbye to all my friends and start all over again in another school. I'm good and grown up then. It's not fair, Mum. Tear up the letter if you want, but I'm not going to write it all over again, so there.'

Julie flung herself out of the room and hurtled up the narrow ladder to the loft. All the good feelings which had come since Callum and she made friends disappeared.

No puppy, no father, no friends except for silly, giggling twins and a boy who couldn't walk beyond the flat pathway to the Place.

What good had praying done? Nothing. 'God isn't a magician,' Callum had said. Of course, she recalled, Dad's present had arrived. Her party dress. She opened her cupboard door. The dress rustled as its folds sprang out of its confined place. There was a tiny gravy stain down the front, but luckily Mum hadn't noticed it.

Yes, it was a beautiful, rich dress. But what was the use of a party dress when there weren't any parties to wear it to?

Only school. A new school. Callum would probably ignore her and be silly with Paul and the other boys, and the twins would stick together as usual.

Then Julie heard the clip-clop of hooves along the drive.

'It's Callum. He's got a horse. Lucky thing!'

But then she realised that Callum couldn't ride alone. His father was guiding the horse. They reined in outside Julie's back door. Callum slithered down from the horse, reached up and patted its tossing nose.

'Okay?' his father asked.

'Aye . . . thanks, Dad.' He took his sticks from his father who swung up into the saddle, not bothering with the shortened stirrups. Callum disappeared under the eaves.

Then there was a knock at the back door.

'Julie,' called her mother, 'It's Callum for you.'

She rushed down the ladder.

'Hi, Callum, was that your own horse?'

'No, we borrow him sometimes.'

'Can't you ride on our own, then?'

He shook his head. 'There's not enough feeling in my legs.'

'I suppose you need strong legs to grip on with,' she agreed. 'Do you want to come in? Mum's busy getting ready for the party tonight. You're all coming, and so are Paul and the twins and their mum and dad.'

'Are you busy too?'

'No, I've been writing my thank you letters.'

'Dad wondered if you'd like to come out with us in the car.'

'Where will we go?'

'Just around . . . the sea, maybe.'

'That's very kind of you, Jim,' said Mrs Murray as she waited to wave them off a little later.

'We won't be away long. There's so little daylight at this time of year.'

'But it's beautiful. In town the winter always seems so dark and grey. I must tell my husband what he's missing. Perhaps we'll persuade him to come home. It's all a question of jobs, of course.'

Julie overheard. 'I hope Dad comes home. I'm going to pray that he will,' she thought.

Jim Brown caught a glimpse of her face in the driving mirror. 'Are you settling in now?'

'Yes, thank you.' But really she felt quite shy, sitting beside Callum in the back of his father's car.

'Well, we're glad you've come, aren't we, Dad?' said Callum.

Julie's spirits lifted when she heard that and she began to enjoy the drive. The car swung along empty roads between pine forests and bare hills until in the end they parked beside moorland and a wide sandy bay.

'Imagine going to the seaside on Boxing Day!' exclaimed Julie.

Dr Brown laughed. 'You're nice to take places,' he said, 'You take such an interest in everything.'

'Mrs Mack was like that too. I'm sure you would have liked her,' Callum said.

'What was she like?' Julie helped push Callum in his wheelchair down to the shore.

'She's the only grown-up I know who's smaller than me,' Callum's voice jerked as the wheelchair jolted. 'You used to say she was like a sparrow, didn't you, Dad? Perhaps that's why the baby blackbird I found reminded me of her.'

But now they had to push hard to keep the wheelchair from sticking in the sand.

'Made it!' Dr Brown exclaimed and Julie ran ahead.

The wind tore her hair. The sea foamed at her feet. Blue islands floated against racing clouds. Words formed inside her head:

*Wind, islands, sea*

*are wise men three*
*bringing Christmas gifts to me.*

She sang those words to herself as she turned cartwheels across the sand to the applause of Callum and his father.

'I love it here! Listen, I've made up a song.'

'Well done, Julie! What Christmas presents do you think your three wise men are bringing you?' Jim Brown pushed the wheelchair towards the sea.

'The wind, the islands and the sea,' repeated Julie. 'They *are* the presents, Dr Brown.'

'And what better presents does anyone need?' the vet agreed.

'Listen, I've made up another verse,' said Callum:

*Wind, islands, sea*
*bring gifts to me.*
*I'm in a chair,*
*but my heart flies free.*

'And I'm as glad as I can be!' added his father. 'Who's for a swim?'

'Not me! You don't really mean it, do you?' asked Julie.

'No, we'd freeze! We swim here in the summer, though. We push the chair right to the edge of the sea,' Dr Brown explained. 'It's a funny thing, Julie, sand seems nice and flat, but you try walking over it if you have anything wrong with your feet or legs, and you'll find it's just impossible.'

'Don't you mind?' Julie asked Callum. 'I mean, I can run about and you can't. I felt jealous when I saw you riding that horse today. Aren't you jealous of me?'

'Not really.' Callum tried to work it out. 'I guess I'm happy being me. I suppose Mum and Dad could easily have decided not to have me.'

Julie hadn't thought of that.

'Lots of people are handicapped in one way or another,' Dr Brown said. 'If the muscles in your eyes don't work properly you have to wear glasses. What's the difference between seeing aids on your nose or walking aids on your feet?'

'Some children have to wear a brace to make their teeth grow straight,' Julie pointed out.

'Exactly. And some people have just as much problem with their temper as Callum does with his legs. What about shyness?' Dr Brown went on. 'I used to be so shy I had to force myself to get on with people, just like Callum had to learn to make his bladder work. I didn't have anything to help me. . . . Perhaps that's why I work with animals,' he added, pushing the wheelchair back towards the path.

'Maybe it's why you get on well with us,' said Julie.

'That's a compliment, Julie.'

'You like old stones so much too,' said Callum. 'Are we taking Julie to see the old stone cross?'

'If she'd like to.'

'Where is it?' asked Julie.

'Inside that little building like a church over there. Here we are. Can you open the door, Julie? Thanks!'

She lifted the latch. The building smelt musty. It was full of old gravestones. Right in the middle stood a stone cross. Its surface was round, like a grandfather clock, between stone supports, and a picture was carved in the stone. Julie went closer to see.

'Is that Jesus hanging on his cross?' she asked, and although the place was empty she lowered her voice.

'Yes. Now look the other side, Julie, along the shaft of the cross. What do you see?'

'That's a deer, isn't it, and a man with an axe. And dogs. What are they doing?'

'They're hunting the deer.'

'They're going to kill it, aren't they? Just like they killed Jesus,' said Julie.

From the other side of the cross Callum said, 'Jesus is handicapped too. He can't move at all because of the nails.'

'I don't like it here,' Julie said. 'It's fusty and smelly. I want to go outside.'

Had she been rude?

'It wasn't that I didn't like the cross,' she tried to explain. 'It was killing . . . the poor deer. Jesus.'

'Too much pain, was there?' asked Dr Brown and he slipped his arm round her shoulders.

'I prefer it out in the open air,' she explained.

'With the wind and the sea? What was your little song? Sing it again.'

So Julie sang:

*Wind, islands, sea*
*are wise men three*
*bringing Christmas gifts to me.*

And Callum added,

*Wind, islands, sea*
*bring gifts to me.*
*I'm in a chair,*
*but my heart flies free.*

'And I'm as glad as I can be. . . . Glad to be us,' Dr Brown added, parking the chair beside the car. 'We're all looking forward to the Christmas party in your house tonight.'

But before the party Callum and Julie checked the bale of hay and went back to the Place to rearrange their stable scene. Then Julie hurried home to help her mother set the table for their guests that night.

# 7

## An important find

That night low lamps and firelight shone on the group of new friends as they circled the table, filling glasses and plates.

'Why don't you young people take your plates up to Julie's room?' suggested Mrs Murray. 'The heating's on, and Julie has records and tapes.'

So up the narrow stairs they went. It was a bit of an effort to get themselves and their laden plates safely to the top, but Dr Brown came to their aid, and Callum went up on his bottom. Upstairs, once they'd eaten and refilled their plates, the boys played with some of Julie's boxed games and the girls experimented with hair-styles, nail varnish and eye make-up.

The twins copied everything Julie did.

They're too young for me, Julie thought again, I wonder if I'll find a friend at school. Still, it was nice to feel she could show the twins something.

'You look like Red Indians,' Paul jeered. 'And what have you done to your hair?'

'Brushed it back, or something,' said Callum. 'It's nice.'

'I can't think why girls waste so much time on all that rubbish!'

'What about the rubbish you boys waste your time on?' retorted Susan.

'Getting muddy and tearing your clothes,' added Claire. 'Don't bother with them, Julie. Do you think I've got this blusher on right?'

'Let's see?' Susan held up a mirror. But Julie turned to Callum.

'I *did* like that cross this afternoon,' she said.

'Which cross?' asked Paul.

'In a ruined chapel by the sea,' Julie told him.

'Never seen it,' said Paul. 'One old stone's like another – boring.'

'How do you know it was boring if you haven't seen it?' asked Julie.

Behind Paul's back Callum shook his head and Julie guessed he didn't want to talk about the cross, especially as he changed the subject, saying, 'Do you want a game?'

'It's my game anyway,' Julie pointed out.

'So it is! Well, shall we all play?'

'I want to show Mum my make-up,' said Claire.

The rest began the game, and of course, soon Claire wanted to join in.

'It's too late, we've started,' said Julie.

'But I want to play too. It's not fair!'

'You'll spoil the game,' said Paul.

'Go on, let me join in.'

'Wait till we've finished this round,' said Callum. 'Then you can play too.'

Mrs Laidlaw called from the bottom of the stairs, Susan! Cla-ire, Paul! Time to go.'

'You'd better get off home too, Callum,' said his mother. 'I'll be over in a minute to help you, but we'll just give Valerie a hand with the dishes.'

'No, you will not! There's no need for that at all.'

But Dr Brown was already in the kitchen and his wife was hurrying to and fro. 'What about the dishes upstairs?' she asked.

'I'll get them,' Julie offered. As she walked back through the room she heard her mother say, 'Thank you for all your help. I'll certainly think over what you said about the job.'

The job? thought Julie, but Jean Brown was saying, 'As I said this afternoon, one thing about having Callum was learning to take one step at a time. And being glad about little things,' she added.

'Like his progress?' asked Julie's mother. 'But Callum's marvellous. . . .'

Julie carried the plates through to the kitchen. 'More dishes is it?' asked Dr Brown. 'Just put them on the side, Julie. I'll do them in a moment.'

'I think there are still some more dirty plates on the table. Shall I get them too?'

Her mother was putting crystal away. Callum's mother paused at the door. 'We believe that God brings good things out of trouble. We shall pray for you and your husband. Perhaps things will work out for him to come back home.'

But then they noticed Julie.

'Have you kids had a nice party too? You certainly look lovely in that gorgeous dress.'

And Julie didn't know what to reply.

'Thanks, Jean,' her mother said for her. 'Julie, you'd better get ready for bed. And I'll go and help Jim finish off those dishes.'

But Julie lingered beside the fire.

'Dear God, please bring Dad home,' she prayed.

Above the noise of dishes she heard snatches of talk from the kitchen. 'Bruce, yes . . . I felt all along . . . something wrong. Jean's talk this afternoon . . . an immense help,' that was her mother's voice.

'Painful . . . a difficult time. God pulled us through.' That was Callum's father. 'Julie . . . a sensitive girl,' his voice went on '. . . needs her father.'

Julie's face went hot. She tiptoed up to bed. Sensitive. That's what her mother had called Callum. Full of feeling. Too much pain was there? 'Jesus is handicapped too. He can't move at all because of those nails.' That's what Callum had said; Callum, who had said sorry to her and shared the Place which she had tried to knock down. Her thoughts whirled round: Callum's disabled legs, the lonely figure on the cross, the dogs and the deer carved in stone . . . but *our* deer are all right.'

She heard the voices downstairs saying goodnight and then, unusually, her mother came up to say goodnight.

'What was that about a job?' Julie asked.

'A job? Oh, well, it's just that when you were out this afternoon, Jean popped in to give me a hand with the food. She really *is* kind, isn't she? We got talking, and, of course, as mothers do, we chatted about our children!'

'About Callum? Or about me?'

'About both of you. I asked about Callum's disabilities, of course, and I told Jean how upset you are by our move. Jean said she and her husband felt concerned about us, you because you're missing Dad so much and me, because . . . well, because of Bruce. Oh, Julie, perhaps I shouldn't be telling you all this, but I've got to talk to someone. I built so much up . . . uprooted us both. You see, I thought perhaps I could build a new life with Bruce.'

Julie shrank back against the pillows. 'That's why you brought me here. I knew it all along.'

'Jean told me quite openly that Bruce has a bad name here. He's not someone to be trusted.'

'I never liked him,' pronounced Julie.

'I know you didn't. I had doubts too. But I was lonely and . . . it's not worth going into all the details now, but it shook me when you mentioned Bruce in your letter to Dad. Julie, I can't send that letter.'

'But it's my thank-you letter.'

'No, but listen, we'll phone him instead. It's expensive, I know, but we'll do it. You see, it would upset him to read about Bruce. I'll explain it all to him when I see him.'

'You mean, Dad really will be coming home?'

'Perhaps, and that's where the job comes in. New offices have just opened in Fynestown. A whole new project is expanding. There might well be a good job for Dad. That's something I can tell him about on the phone. And there'll certainly be a secretary's job for me,

Jim said. So I won't need to count on Bruce. Does that make you any happier?'

'Mm, I think so,' said Julie, and when her mother finally went away Julie got up, switched on the light and pulled out the doll Bruce had given her.

'Stupid doll. I've always hated you! Even the twins wouldn't look twice at you.'

She shoved the doll into her waste-paper basket, carried the basket downstairs to the kitchen and tiptoed back to bed. Suddenly she remembered. She sat bolt upright and folded her hands 'Thank you,' she told God. 'Lots and lots of love. I really mean it. Julie.'

Next morning her mother found the doll.

'Julie, what's this? That's the doll from Br . . . ' she checked herself. 'It wasn't a very suitable present for someone of your age, was it? But it seems a shame to throw it away. Jean tells me that she and Callum are going to hospital in a day or two. . . . '

'Hospital? Is Callum all right?'

'It's only for a check-up. It's a good thing the frost has melted. Perhaps Jean can give the doll to one of the children's wards.'

'All right.'

Immediately after breakfast Julie went off to find Callum. 'Let's go to the Place. I want to see our crib and I want to tell you something.'

'Okay, but we mustn't be long.'

'Why not?'

'There's a dyker coming. Mr McLaren, he's called.'

'What's a dyker?'

'He mends walls. I want to watch.'

'I'll watch him too. Will Paul be coming?'

'Not till later. . . . Right, I'm ready.'

The winter sun threw their shadows across the path. Callum gave the hay a close inspection. 'It's been nibbled at. Paul said he'd get us more.'

'What about the crib people? Look, they're wet.'

'Perhaps we'd better take them home. The cows will

be back soon and they'll spoil them.'

'And Christmas Day is over. It's been a good Christmas, though.'

They settled beside the hearth.

'I'd like us to pray now,' said Julie, and she explained, 'Mum's getting a job in Fynestown, we hope. And there might be one for Dad. I believe Jesus can help my mum and dad, just like he helps your family.' Julie hesitated. 'It's all happened because you said sorry to me that time, when it was really my fault,' she explained. 'I want to say sorry to you too.'

'What for?'

'I wobbled a stone in the chimney. I didn't mean to the first time. But when I was mad with you I wanted to knock the Place down. . . . Of course, I couldn't, but I think a stone got loose. Look, in here.'

Callum probed the fireplace with his hands.

'Mm, I can feel it wobble. But it doesn't matter, Julie. The fireplace is still standing.'

'You don't think the whole chimney will fall down?'

'It might one day, but do you know something? We can ask Mr McLaren, the dyker.'

'That means we'll have to show him the Place.'

'Yes, but that doesn't matter if he helps us get it fixed . . .'

'So you don't mind? I've felt so bad about it, Callum. I was frightened to tell you because I thought you wouldn't want to be friends with me any more.'

'Oh, Julie. . . !' Callum supported himself against the fireplace. 'You're a real friend. You understand things.'

'That's all right then. Well, let's talk to God.'

They closed their eyes. The wind sang among the larch trees. Burn water chattered. A lorry rushed by. Small birds chirped. There was a sound of a stone striking on to stone.

It's odd how loud everything gets when we're quiet, Julie thought, but she didn't say anything because she didn't want to disturb the quiet.

'Please help Julie's mum to get a job,' Callum prayed.

'And help Dad too,' added Julie.

'May he know we're thinking of him just now even though he's so far away,' Callum continued.

'And may Mr McLaren mend our Place,' Julie said.

They paused. It was hard work keeping their eyes closed so long in the daytime. 'Am-...' Callum began, but Julie added quickly, 'With lots of love from Julie.'

'And Callum,' added Callum.

They opened their eyes.

'So that's that. We're going to phone Dad tonight. Do you think Mr McLaren's here yet?'

'He might be. I thought I heard the sound of stones being worked.'

'Let's go and see. We'll put the crib figures away first, though.'

So they called at Julie's house and then they went down to the main road where an old man was refitting stones into the wall.

'Good morning, Mr McLaren,' called Callum.

'Well, it's Jim Brown's boy. How are you, son? Are the legs still needing a bit of support?'

'Aye, but I'm fine. This is Julie.'

The old man held out a rough hand, 'You'll be up here for the holidays?'

'No, I live here now, next door to Callum.'

'In Mrs Mack's cottage,' Callum explained.

'Mistress Mack, oh, aye.'

'You knew her then?'

'Lizze and I were at the school together.' He slotted a boulder into place and straightened his back. 'We were born and brought up in the wee houses yonder. Of course there's only ruins there now.'

'There's still a fireplace left standing all by itself. Would you like to come and see?'

'Well, now, that would be interesting right enough.'

'Come in for a cup of coffee on your way,' offered Callum.

'I have a flask with me, but thanks all the same,' the old man pointed to a canvas bag. 'Coffee with three sugars. They say sugar's bad for you, but I've survived long enough,' he chuckled. 'Come away then. I'm no' paid to inspect fireplaces, but I'll be glad to have a look for old time's sake.'

'We think there's a stone loose inside.' By now they were walking between fallen stones to the Place, and the old man became full of memories.

'How times change!' he said. 'I mind all the folks here, and they're all dead, or away. There was no higher education for the likes of us. But Lizzie had a great memory. She knew things about this place that historians and archae . . . thae folk who dig up old bones. . . .'

'Archaeologists,' suggested Callum.

'Aye, them. That they'd be glad tae ken. Now, let's have a wee look at your chimney.'

'The loose stone's right inside,' said Julie, but the old man wasn't to be hurried, as he eased his body with its layers of bulky clothing into the hearth.

'What's this then? Here's the loose stone, right enough. It's been dislodged someway. But it's set against the very cornerstone, and do you ken what I think? Someone has slipped a gey auld* bit of rock into this chimney. Shall I take it out for you to see?'

'So long as the whole chinney doesn't collapse,' said Callum.

'No, son, you're safe enough. These stones are too well set together, but I tell you what, why don't you young ones find me a stone that will fit?' He sketched with his thick fingers the size of stone they should find and Callum and Julie went off in search of it. Julie plunged among ruts and boulders while Callum stayed on the path, pushing his sticks around the overgrown field at the edge of the pathway.

'I've found one!' exclaimed Julie, 'but it's stuck.'

* gey auld = very old

'Have my sticks,' Callum sat on the ground.

'It's all right. I've got it. Will this one do, Mr McLaren?' She tried to hold it up. 'Oh, it's too heavy, and now I'm all covered in mud.'

'Wait your hurry, wait your hurry,' the old man came to her rescue. 'Aye, that stone's fine, and now, see what I've found in your chimney.'

He held out an old stone which was criss-crossed with curving lines.

'They're like the patterns on the stone cross we saw,' said Julie, 'Callum, that stone must be really old.'

'Oh aye, it's old right enough,' said Mr McLaren.

They sat on the ground examining the find while Mr McLaren fitted the replacement stone into the chimney and made their fireplace secure.

'Perhaps we'll get a reward,' Julie said.

'Your father will be interested in yon,' Mr McLaren told Callum.

'Must we show it to him?' said Julie, 'It's ours, isn't it?'

'No, lassie,' the old man said, 'It was here in this glen long before you came.'

'It could be a clue,' said Callum. 'Mrs Mack said there would be silver, you see.'

'Let me hold it again,' said Julie.

Callum put the stone between her hands. It was too heavy to hold for long. She set it on the ground and traced its patterns with her fingers.

'You're right, Mr McLaren, the stone does belong here, and holding it makes me feel as though I belong as well.'

'And so you do,' Callum assured her.

'But why do you think they used this stone to build their fireplace?'

'Who knows?' the old man said. 'Lizzie Mack maybe knew something about it, but it's been left for you young ones to discover.' He picked up his bag. 'I'll away. I'm here to mend dykes, not do your archaeol – . . . whatever it is.'

'We'll tell you what Dad says about the stone,' promised Callum. 'Just think, Julie, this would never have happened if you hadn't found the Place.'

'I wobbled the stones because I lost my temper. Mum said something yesterday about good coming out of bad. I never thought it would happen so soon.'

'Our hidden treasure! I wonder what Mrs Mack would say?'

'Quite a lot, I should think,' his mother said when she heard the story, and his father said, 'I think this will turn out to be a most important find. We'll have to send this stone away to be examined, of course, but it seems to me that it's part of a much bigger thing.'

And Callum and Julie were sure that Dr Brown was right, but what that bigger thing could be, of course, they had no idea.

# 8

## 'I am your friend'

'What's all the fuss about?' said Paul. 'It's only an old stone.'

'But it's an *antique*,' said Claire.

'It's a sort of buried treasure,' said Susan. 'Let me hold it next.'

'It's a wonderful find,' said Julie's mother. 'We'll tell Dad all about it.'

'We must tell him about your job too,' said Julie.

'Yes, I'm starting next week. We'll phone Dad tonight.'


'Dad, is it really you? It's Julie. Yes, I can hear you fine. There's a bit of a humming sound. Do you think it's the sea? Thank you for your Christmas present. Guess what? I'm having my photo in the papers. So's Callum. It's all because of an old stone we found. Dad, do you miss us?'

And over the phone Julie heard her father say, 'Miss you? Of course I do, Julie.'

'Let me speak now, Julie,' her mother said, so Julie handed over the phone.

'I'm glad I wore Dad's dress for the photographs. We'll have to send him copies so's he can see what it looks like on me,' she said as they discussed the call afterwards.

But when the photographs were printed in three different papers they just showed Julie's face.'

'Still, they're lovely of you and Callum, and what a nice smile old Mr McLaren has.'

'He has three spoons of sugar in his coffee. Mum, it's such a shame Callum's away to hospital today. He won't see the pictures till he gets home this evening.'

'I tell you who will see them, Julie. Your new teachers and the other children. Perhaps that will make it easier for you starting school. It's only two days from now.'

A new white shirt and grey skirt hung in Julie's bedroom already.

And the thought of everything ahead of her made Julie wander alone towards the Place.

It was colder today. She wouldn't stay long. She knelt beside the hearth and listened to all the sounds you only hear when you become quiet.

'Can you see me down here, God? I want you to be with Callum in hospital today. Please help me when I start school. Lots of love, Julie.'

She stood up, but she didn't feel like leaving the Place.

Supposing God wants to speak back, like Dad on the phone.

The wind sang in the forest. Grey clouds covered the sky. There were footprints all round the Place and a scattering of loose stones.

Julie waited, listening, in case God wanted to say something. All she heard was silence, but in that silence God seemed to be saying to her, 'I am your friend.' I know you are, thought Julie and now she didn't need to wait any longer in the Place. She turned away, put on her disco boots and skated down to Ballonoch Farm to play with the twins.

'It wasn't an actual voice, of course,' she explained to Callum in the Place next day. 'I just felt that God was there. I'm sure he will be with me when we start school.'

'I'm sure he will be,' said Callum. 'You know, Julie, I didn't want you to come and live here instead of Mrs Mack, but I'm glad about it now.'

'So am I,' Julie agreed, 'and do you know what the twins said? There should be puppies for sale soon.'

'Puppies for sale,' sighed her mother.

'Mum, you promised.'

'But I'm starting work. I shall have to come home at lunch times if we have a puppy.'

'It's not far,' said Julie, 'not in the car. Please, Mum, you said we could have a dog. And I haven't been complaining about coming here and missing all my friends.'

'No, but then look at all the nice things that have happened. It's not everyone who makes a rare archaeological discovery. And from all accounts there may be more discoveries in store.'

'The dog can help us find them,' argued Julie.

'That's wishful thinking. . . . How did Callum get on at hospital?'

'Fine, but he's to have an operation soon. On his feet. They're going to cut his tendons. Callum says it's only a small operation, but I'd hate to have my feet cut open.'

'Why does he need it done?'

'To stop his feet turning in so much.'

'I see.' Mrs Murray slipped her arm round Julie's shoulders. 'I'm glad you're such a kind-hearted girl, dear, and I'm so glad you're happier these days. I look at your nice smiling photograph in the paper and I feel very proud of you.'

And Julie felt the same kind of quiet happiness she had found in the Place when God seemed so close to her.


After that going to school wasn't so bad.

'How did you get on?' Mrs Murray asked as they ate their evening meal on the first day of term.

'Fine,' smiled Julie. 'Everyone said, "Are you Callum's friend?". Or, "Are you the girl who found the stone?" '

'It's a nice small school.'

'Yes, but it's funny having so many different ages in one class.'

'New things always take time getting used to. I'm having to learn new things at work too, and meet new people.'

The door bell rang. It was Dr Brown.

'I'm sorry to disturb you at your meal, but I thought you'd like to know that there's an archaeologist coming round some time to look at the place where the stone was found.'

'They won't take the fireplace apart, will they?'

'No, I'm sure they won't. There aren't any funds available, they say, to finance any further digs.'

'Would you like a coffee, Jim? We're just about to have one.'

'Then I'll be glad to join you. How was school, Julie?'

'Fine,' nodded Julie.

'Callum told us you got star treatment! That's great. And did you have a good day, Valerie?'

'Busy,' Mrs Murray put mugs of coffee on the table. 'But I like it better that way. Do you think that the stone is quite valuable, Jim?'

'Very likely. The archaeologists are suggesting that it might be part of a cross.'

'A big cross, like the one we saw beside the sea?' Julie asked.

'Probably every bit as big as that one, and covered with carvings too. Just think, Julie,' Dr Brown sipped his coffee. 'Long before anyone built our houses here, or even the tumble-down ones where Mrs Mack once lived, there would have been people in Ballonoch, children playing. . . .'

'And deer,' added Julie.

'Oh yes, certainly some deer. And Christian missionaries would have come, monks whose undyed woollen robes would seem very plain to the village folk here who loved bright colours and made their own dyes.'

'You make it all seem like yesterday, Jim, but it was very long ago, wasn't it?' Valerie Murray said.

'About a thousand years or so.'

'So the monks built the cross?' Valerie went on.

'Oh yes. They lived in simple huts, but they would make sure the best stone carvers and artists built their cross.'

'What a lot we'll have to write to your dad about, Julie!'

'How is your husband?'

'We phoned him the other day,' said Julie. 'He said he'd write to us, but the letter hasn't come yet. But the twins say they'll be having puppies soon. We're going to get one, aren't we, Mum?'

'Oh dear, yes, I suppose we are.'

The grown ups laughed with that sort of agreeing with one another which adults often seem to have. Dr Brown drained his cup. 'That was very nice, thank you. Well, Julie, I'm glad school went well. And don't be surprised if you find an archaeologist at the door wanting to chat with you one of these days.'

But it was two months before an archaeologist came, and of course a lot of things happened before that.

One thing was a flurry of letters between Ballonoch and Yaristan which ended with Julie running across to find Callum.

'Come to the Place. I've got good news.'

He seized his sticks at once. 'Come on then.'

Their breath blew smoke signals into the February air.

'Dad's coming home,' Julie announced. 'for good.'

'That *is* good news. When?'

'In September, probably. It's so far away I can hardly think about it. We'll be at secondary school, won't we?'

'Aye, travelling in by bus. What's your dad going to do?'

'Work in the new project in Fynestown. Callum, I want to say thank you to God. I've said it already at home, but I want you to share the thank you too.'

'I think we should get our recorders and play a thank you song.'

'But I can only play "In the light of the moon" and "London's Burning", and I can't get all the notes, either.'

'All right,' Callum relented. 'Let's bring our recorders here another time though.'

So instead of playing their recorders, they listened to the burn, to rooks in the trees, to the wind and to the cows mooing and coughing on the hill.

'Thank you, God,' said Julie. 'I wanted Dad to come home so much and now it's happening.'

'Please give Julie's dad a safe journey home. No hijacks or anything,' added Callum.

'Lots of love from us both,' Julie ended.

Callum stood up. 'I've got to go now.'

'Where to?'

'Paul's to watch *Ace Riders*.'

'Would you like me to push you in your wheelchair?'

'I was just going to walk.'

'But there's not much time before the programme and your feet aren't working so well until you get your operation. I heard your mum say so.'

'I'll be all right.'

'No, Callum . . . I tell you what. I'll push the chair back on its own and you can walk home when the programme's finished.'

But in the end the twins invited Julie to watch *Ace Riders* too, so Callum got a ride both ways.

'The puppies will be born in about two weeks,' said the twins and they hustled Julie off to see the mother-to-be, a honey-coloured labrador.

'Isn't she fat?'

'So would you be with babies inside you,' giggled the twins.

'I wonder how many she'll have? They usually have six or seven puppies, don't they? Imagine having six babies all at once!'

'Mum says twins are bad enough,' they told Julie, 'But we're glad we're twins.'

'I often wish I had a sister,' said Julie.

After the programme they had juice and cakes, then Julie pushed Callum's wheelchair home in the dark.

The headlights of oncoming cars picked up the luminous strips which were stuck on to Callum's wheelchair. He flashed a bike lamp ahead of them to light up the way.

They arrived home to hear the news: 'Dr Dickson phoned.'

'Who's he?'

'She, not he. An archaeologist. She's coming to see you after school tomorrow.'

'I wonder what she'll be like?' said Julie. Dr Dickson was red-headed, with enormous glasses and heavy jewellery.

'Hullo,' she greeted the children. 'I recognise you from your photographs.'

'Have you still got our stone?' asked Julie.

'Yes. I can't be parted from it!'

'We didn't want to give it away, either,' said Julie under her breath.

'It's a wonderful find,' Dr Dickson enthused, directing her talk to Dr Brown who had come home early to see her. 'Quite primitive . . . carved stones . . . tenth or twelfth century.'

While she talked, Julie and Callum looked at their stone again.

'So it's been part of a cross which was made about a thousand years ago. Look, you kids, you can see how it fitted into place.' Dr Brown tried to include the children in the archaeologist's talk.

'Do you think there was a church here once?' asked Julie, 'or just a cross standing all by itself?'

But Dr Dickson went on talking. 'We'd love to carry out a full investigation on the site, but there aren't any funds. We'll have the stone classified and it will go into the National Museum. Of course, you children will receive a letter of thanks. Now, if you could just show me where you found the stone. . . '

'But that will mean taking the fireplace apart like Mr McLaren did,' objected Callum.

'Mr McLaren?'

'An old man who mends drystone walls,' explained Dr Brown. 'He actually found the stone.'

'Ah, yes, . . . so would you like to show me the way?'

'Up here,' Dr Brown pointed.

'Fascinating, just that chimney left. In here, you said?' Dr Dickson snapped her camera briskly to record the site. 'I suppose we'd better write and thank Mr McLaren too. And now, thank you very much. It's been really delightful meeting you.'

And she drove away.

'With *our* stone,' said Julie. 'It's not fair.'

'I'm glad you didn't tell her about the hidden treasure Mrs Mack talked about, Dad?'

'It was on the tip of my tongue, but I could see she didn't really want to listen.'

'I wish we could have kept our stone,' said Julie.

'Think of the schoolchildren who'll get taken to see it in the museum,' Dr Brown began.

'Aye, and if they're like Paul, they'll just think it's boring,' Callum pointed out.

'They'll never know it was *our* hidden treasure,' said Julie.

'They'll be told that two children found it,' said Dr Brown. 'Some children might be interested in your story.'

# 9

## Puppies, exhibits, letters

A few days later, on a wet Saturday, Callum was playing his recorder.

'That's a different sort of sound,' his mother remarked. 'Deeper. Easier to listen to.'

'Aye, it's called a tenor recorder. The teacher's lent it to me.'

'Perhaps you'll be able to borrow a flute when you go to secondary school.'

'I like this recorder. But I wish I had more music. Could we go to a music shop some time?'

'Yes, but you should be hearing about your hospital appointment soon. Maybe we can find a music shop when we go to Glasgow. Meantime, I'll have to keep on doing my dusting to the *Skye Boat Song*.'

'It's *Greensleeves* today,' said Callum, 'but the low notes are difficult to blow.'

The door bell rang as Callum tried to blow bottom D sharp.

'Hullo, Paul,' he heard his mother say. 'What a wet day! Let me take your waterproof.'

Paul's face appeared round the door as he tugged himself free of his dripping jacket. 'The dog's had her puppies,' he announced.

'D, D, C sharp, B . . . has she? We'd better tell Julie, but I'll just clean out my recorder.'

'Why don't you run next door, Paul, and tell Julie, while Callum gets himself ready. You'll need the waterproof cover if you go out in your chair.'

73

'How many has she had?' Callum called after Paul's retreating back.

'Five. All honey like her.'

'Oh, they're *sweet*!' Julie enthused as they pushed the wheelchair into the shed. 'Can we hold them?'

The twins dived expertly among the squeaking puppies and Julie tried to soothe a little wriggling body in her arms.

'There's one for us all,' Susan said, putting a puppy on Callum's knee.

'Hey, what's this? Good thing the cover's still on the chair,' Callum observed as a puddle formed. 'Got a cloth?'

'Ugh!' giggled the twins, but Callum held the puppy against him with one hand and wiped up its mess with a cloth Paul threw across to him.

The mother watched them carefully, her ears pricked.

'She's certainly keeping a watchful eye on us,' said Julie. 'I don't want to put my puppy down, but I suppose we'd better let her have them back.'

Soon the wriggling pups were back beside their mother.

'When do you think I can get mine?'

'Not for six weeks,' Susan said.

'Which one do you want?' asked Claire.

'I don't know . . . they're all sweet. Look how greedy they are, yet they're so tiny. See their wee tails. They're just perfect. . . . '

'Don't you wish you were having one?' she asked Callum as she pushed the wheelchair home.

'In a way. But Mum doesn't like dogs. Too much mess, she says. And it would be a problem taking one for a walk.'

'I'll take my dog for lots of walks. I won't mind at all,' said Julie. 'I'll go over the hills. It's a pity you won't be able to come with us, though.'

'I might, when I'm thirteen.'

'Why, what's happening when you're thirteen?'

'I might be getting a trike with a motor which can go over rough ground.'

'That'll be good.'

'Aye. I'll be able to race everyone up all the hills!'

'Except the dog. Dogs run fast.'

'Perhaps not the dog,' Callum agreed, 'but everyone else. It will be great seeing what's over the hill where the deer live.'

'We've not been putting out any hay – not since school started.'

'Dad says it doesn't matter. It's not been frosty enough. But the forecast says there's cold weather on the way. Paul's dad said we could have more hay.'

'We haven't been to the Place either. In fact, I've hardly seen you. What have you been doing?'

'Playing my recorder,' Callum explained.

It was true. Recorder playing filled hours at a time. Callum blew till his mouth felt dry.

'Anyone else would run out of breath, or patience,' his mother said. 'All you seem to run out of is music.'

'Dad's going to get me some next time he's in Oban.'

'That's good because the hospital appointment isn't till April. We'll all be fed up with *Greensleeves* by then!'

*23rd February.*

*Dear Dad,*

*How are you? It's snowing here. Callum and me made a snowman. We tried to make a snowchair, but we couldn't. I made a snow puppy. The puppy I'm getting is much nicer. I'm calling her Sarna. That's a name I read in a book. It means "deer". It's Polish. We put out hay for the deer, you see. I'm sure Sarna knows me, but she's still with her mother. The puppies are all sweet. They run all over the barn and try to chew our toes.*

*Our stone is going on show in the museum soon and we've all been invited to go and see it. Callum and his Dad are certain there are more old things here, perhaps* even some treasure. They want to show me an old bell in the museum in Edinburgh in case there are more things like it in Ballonoch.

Mum says that we might be able to have an outing to Edinburgh with you when you come home. Then you can see our stone in the museum, but September seems a long way away.

Lots of love,

*Julie*

P.S. Those blobs are meant to be snowballs. Do you like the puppies at the bottom of the page?


                                        12th March
Dear Dad,

How are you? Mum and me are counting the days till you come home.

The snow melted after I wrote. There are lots of snowdrops. When the wind blows they look like lambs.

Sarna belongs to me now. I could fill this whole letter with news of her. She's gorgeous. She chews up everything she can find. She hates it when we go to Fynestown and leave her behind, but we can't take her yet because she hasn't had her injections.

We're going to Edinburgh tomorrow to see the stone.

Mum's taking the day off work and so are Callum's mum and dad. We're leaving at 8 o'clock. I'm going to wear the dress you gave me. The twins have promised to look after Sarna and give her walks before and after school. We've left them a doorkey.

Lots of love,

*Julie,*

P.S. I shall send you a photo of Sarna soon. I've nearly finished my film.


'Are you kids okay in the back?'

'Aye, we're fine. I'm glad I took off my calipers though. It's much comfier without them.'

'How about you, Jean?' Julie's mother asked from the front seat. 'Are you sure you won't change your mind and sit here instead of me?'

'Not at all. I'll probably do some driving later on.'

'I hope Sarna's all right,' said Julie as the car swung by Ballonoch Farm.

'Of course she will be. Look, there go Susan and Claire on their way to give Sarna a walk. You must buy them a bar of chocolate in Edinburgh, Julie, to say thank you.'

The car ate up the miles of empty road.

'Can you go faster, Dad?' Callum bounced on the back seat.

'Steady on, Cal, I'm not a rally driver!'

'Why do you want to go so fast?' wondered Julie, 'I get car sick.'

'Oh dear, Julie, Dr Brown is doing his best,' her mother told her.

'Well, let's open the window. It's just I like it when the car goes fast. Pity wheelchairs don't do ninety miles an hour.'

'It's just as well they don't,' his father interrupted. 'You can have that window open so long as there's no draught. And, Julie, I promise you I'll go really slow when the road gets twisty. Tell you what, would you like your Top Forty cassette on now?'

Pop music took them eastwards to Edinburgh.

Once they were inside the museum they found their stone easily. It sat on a pillar all by itself, highlighted by special lighting.

'Ballonoch carved stone,' said a card beside it. 'Found in a ruined chimney by Angus McLaren, Julie Murray and Callum Brown.'

'That's us!' exclaimed Julie, 'look, everyone, and look how nice the stone is now it's been cleaned up, You can see the twisting patterns much more clearly.'

A photographer took pictures of Callum and Julie

standing beside their stone. 'For our files,' the director of the museum explained. 'Your stone is already catalogued. No, we still can't be precise about its date. . . . Now, let's show you round the museum and then we invite you to a buffet lunch upstairs in the library.'

Julie's mind became a confused whirl of glassware and jewellery, costumes worn by ladies long ago, the guillotine which cut peoples' heads off, bones and beakers, old clocks and brooches and silver chains.

'Worn by Pictish chieftains, we think,' the director said.

'Could we see the bell which was found near Ballonoch?' Callum asked.

'Ah, yes, of course. This way. It's in that case.'

'It's beautiful,' Julie's breath made the glass steamy, 'and do you know something? The carving looks a bit like the spirals on our stone.'

'So it does,' they all agreed.

'Don't you think so?' Dr Brown asked the museum director.

'Do you know, I believe you're right,' he said, peering close. 'Our researchers did a most thorough study, and yet no one seems to have picked this up. I'll go and get Dr Dickson, if you'll excuse me,' and he hurried away.

Julie and Callum pressed their noses close to the glass and peered at the bell.

'Jesus is on his cross, but he's wearing a crown, like a king.' Julie's voice was hushed. 'King Jesus! What a sad face he has. . . .'

Just then the director brought Dr Dickson in to compare the bell and the stone.

'Oh, yes, there are definite similarities between the bell and the children's stone,' she said at once. 'How fascinating. There's a whole new study opening up.'

'That's fine,' the director said, 'but I must take our young discoverers up for lunch.'

A month later a letter arrived from the museum. 'It is most interesting to notice how alike the bell and the

Ballonoch stone are,' it said. 'Further investigations are in hand and we must thank you again for your interest and support.'

But the morning after the museum letter, news arrived from Yaristan for Julie.

> *Yaristan Oil Company*
> *Dhohore*
> *Easter Sunday*

*Dear Julie,*

*Thank you for your letter. Yes, you're right. It's hot all the time here. Sometimes it's cloudy and hot, sometimes it's sunny and hot, sometimes it's humid – but it's always hot. Of course, our buildings are air-conditioned, but outside it's another story.*

*I'm glad Sarna is giving you so much pleasure. Did I ever tell you I think you're good at choosing names? There's a Polish engineer on our project. He was pleased when I told him that my daughter has given her puppy a Polish name.*

*I hope Mum forgave Sarna for chewing up the rug you told me about in your last letter. . . .'*

Oh dear, yes, that was dreadful, Julie recalled, putting down the rustling sheet of airmail paper to fondle Sarna.

*I hope you enjoyed your Easter service in church today. You told me that Callum was playing a solo on his tenor recorder. What kind of instrument is that, I wonder? Perhaps you can draw me one in your next letter. I like your drawings very much. How good it is to think that in only six months I shall be home with you and Mum, and Sarna too, of course.*

*I read your letters over and over again. The things you write about Jesus, your happiness – these all cheer me up more than you can know. So much so that I went to church today. I've almost run out of space, but I'll tell you a bit about it.*

*It was very different from your church – brown faces, bright clothes, a different language. Everyone sits on the floor.*

I sat on the floor at the back. If people were surprised to see a white man in their little church, they were too polite to show it. (Most Europeans, if they go to church at all, travel to town to a service in English). A girl sang a song about Jesus. She would be about your age, but smaller and thinner. Despite the oil, the local economy is poor and these people have only the bare necessities. In fact, I felt ashamed of my lifestyle. I see rich men every day. Their faces are worried. They keep calm on pills and whisky. Those people in church were calm without any of those things.

After the service, instead of going out for dinner and drinks, I stayed in my hotel room. There's a Bible beside the bed. For the first time since coming here I opened it. I didn't know where to begin, but I found the Easter stories, and since then I've found myself praying too. And now I've run completely out of space except to say – Lots of love to you and Mum and Sarna. Dad.

# 10

## A lamb and a secret

'Oh, Sarna,' whispered Julie, 'I wish you could read Dad's letter.'

She re-read it several times and showed it to her mother. 'I wish I could meet that girl. I'd like to invite her here. We could play with Sarna. I could show her the Place. I must tell Callum about her . . .'

And she did.

'It's funny to think that thousands of miles away, right across the world there's a girl of our age who made my dad happy.'

'It makes the place and us seem small,' Callum looked up at the fresh green larches. Then they heard a car engine. 'That's Dad,' said Callum.

'It always amazes me how you can tell whose car it is just from the engine,' said Julie. 'Why do you think he's come home so early?'

'Perhaps he's forgotten something.'

'I'd like to tell him about Dad. I feel he would understand . . . Look, he's waving.'

'Run on ahead then,' said Callum, so Julie did.

'Hi there, Julie, called Dr Brown. 'Ballonoch Farm have phoned. There's a lamb being born. Would you like to come?'

'Oh yes! I'll just put Sarna in the house. She'd better not come, had she?'

'No, not this time.'

'Dr Brown . . . could I show you Dad's letter just quickly?'

'Very quickly then. You get it while I turn the car.'

So Julie took Sarna home and fetched the letter. Dr Brown read it while Callum clambered into the car.

'That's a wonderful letter, Julie. Thank you for letting me read it. I must say I'm looking forward to getting to know your dad. I was very impressed,' he added, driving off, 'when Valerie told us he was taking the Fynestown job, because it obviously means a drop in salary.'

'Yes, but he says here, rich men aren't always happy, but that girl is. I wish I could meet her.'

'You could write a letter to her.'

'But she doesn't speak English. . . . Will the lamb be born yet?'

'I don't know. It's mother seems to be having a bit of a struggle.'

The mother ewe was standing in the yard, bleating.

'We're so glad you've come,' chorused the twins. 'No one can get the lamb out.'

'It seems to be stuck,' Mrs Laidlaw said, 'I've been hanging on, but nothing is happening.'

'Let's have a look. Ah, I see the problem. Its feet should be coming out with its head.'

'Is that its head here?' asked Julie.

'Yes, and its feet are still inside. And it's beginning to panic.'

But how the vet could tell what was happening to the lamb while it was still mostly inside its mother was a mystery to Julie.

'Can you all stand back a bit?' Dr Brown asked.

They stood back, obediently. Above the bleating of the ewe a lark sang as it spiralled upwards in the April air.

Dr Brown thrust his hand into the sheep's body. 'It wants to be born but its feet are acting like brakes. Let's see if a good strong pull will help . . . no, I'm going to have to push the lamb back a bit and see if we can start again. . . . That's it, Paul and Julie, you could hang on to me. Wait till I take my jacket off, though. That's better! Callum and twins, see if you can soothe the poor mum.'

'You'll be all right,' the twins said soothingly, while Dr Brown tugged at the lamb. Paul and Julie slithered in the mud. 'One more tug,' the vet said. 'Look the wee one's coming now. And there we are!'

The children staggered backwards as the lamb was pulled out into the world.

'Well done, everyone.'

'Can we hold the lamb?' begged the twins. 'Look, Julie, she's almost as tiny as Sarna was.'

'No, Sarna was far smaller,' Julie stroked the lamb's wet fleece. 'I feel as if we've all worked hard,' she added.

'And so you have.' Dr Brown was checking the mother sheep. 'There, everything's all right now.'

'Won't you have a cup of tea?' invited Mrs Laidlaw.

'I'd love one, but I'd better not stop. Things are frantic just now. Do you want a lift home, Cal? How about you, Julie?'

'I'd rather stay with the lamb,' said Julie.

'Me too. I'll manage home all right.'

'I'll go with you and if you feel it's taking too long I'll run on for the wheelchair,' said Julie.

'Good idea. Okay then. Look, she's got the right idea, She's starting to feed already. She might limp for a day or two, but she'll thrive. I'd leave them both down beside the farm for a bit,' Dr Brown told Mrs Laidlaw.

'I wonder what it feels like to be born,' Julie said, but Callum and Paul went off to play with the dogs.

'We were all born once,' said the twins, 'but no one remembers.'

'All that blood. It's messy. I wonder how my mum felt.'

'Our mother says her problems only began once we were born,' Claire said. 'Sheep hve twins too. Come on, Julie, let's go and see the other lambs. This one's okay now.'

But before she went home Julie went to visit the new

lamb. It lay beside its mother.

'You're special because I watched you being born. And you matter, even if your legs aren't quite right yet,' she told it. Suddenly she remembered how she had felt when she first met Callum. 'I hated his calipers, but I never notice them now. It was silly being embarrassed. I think it was because I was so unhappy.'

And she thought of the girl far away in Yaristan.

'It doesn't matter whether our bodies work or not,' she said to Callum as they made their slow way home. 'And it doesn't matter whether we're brown or black or white.'

'What does matter then?'

'Being born . . . being us. I'm glad we saw that lamb being born.'

'Me too, but there are loads of lambs. Look at them in the field there.'

They stopped to count the lambs and give Callum a rest.

'Fifteen,' counted Callum.

'No, sixteen,' Julie pointed. 'That one's just come out from underneath its mother. Silly things to be so frightened of us. I love their wriggly tails! No wonder catkins are called lambs' tails. Oh, Callum, you're going to miss all this when you go to Glasgow to hospital next week. Do you know what I've been thinking? I'll plant primroses in the Place.'

'It's not worth it. The cows will trample them to bits.'

'Perhaps I can build a sort of wall.'

'Oh, Julie, they'd soon knock it over.'

'Well, I'll think of something.'

'Like, put up a notice saying, "Keep out cows"!'

'Of course not!'

But still she wondered what to do.

I could always clear the ground a bit, she thought as she walked Sarna up the hill behind the Place. It was a Monday holiday at the end of April. She had just waved

Callum and his mother off to hospital.

'Don't worry, I'll be fine,' Callum said. 'I've got my recorder. Mum's going to buy me heaps of new music.'

'You're very brave,' Julie observed. 'I'd hate to think my legs were going to be cut open.'

'It's not very nice waking up and finding your legs in plaster,' agreed Callum, 'but I know I'll be walking again on sticks before long, so that's okay.'

Julie thought of that as she and Sarna ran over ruts and hummocks of turf.

Before I met Callum I never thought about being disabled. But he's glad about the things he can do. 'Hey, come back, Sarna!'

But the puppy was away, a streak of pale amber, chasing a rabbit. Julie stopped to look at primroses.

It wouldn't be right to dig them up, and the cows would trample them, she thought, but I'll dig up some weeds and put stones in a pattern round the fireplace. I think there are garden tools in the garage.

Her mother was working until three pm and Julie was expected at Ballonoch Farm for her lunch. But until then she could do what she wanted.

And I might as well make the Place look nice.

She fetched the tools and started to dig up the bracken which was beginning to uncurl around the Place.

'This is hard work,' she panted. She sat back on her heels for a rest. Sarna nosed in and started to dig where Julie had been working. 'Go away, Sarna, you're getting in my way.' But Sarna was tired of chasing rabbits, it seemed, and she wanted to dig exactly where Julie was making a hole.

'The more I dig the more Sarna joins in. She's getting deeper and deeper. Stop it, Sarna. There aren't any rabbits down there, you know, and if there were, you'd have frightened them all away by now.'

But Sarna went on digging.

It's a pity Callum's not here to help us, thought Julie, and then she remembered that she had promised herself she would pray for Callum.

'Dear God, help Callum in hospital. Don't let it hurt too much. I'm so glad he's got his recorder. He's got a personal stereo too, and he knows that you're with him even though he can't see you. Lots of love from Julie. . . . Oh, Sarna, that hole is enormous now. Look at your nose! It's all dirty. You must be thirsty too. Do you know, I could almost plant a tree in the hole you've made, except there are enough trees here already. Wait, what's that?'

Deep in the hole Julie noticed a piece of pottery. Wisps of some sort of material flapped around it.

It's a brick. No, it's broken china. Someone's broken teapot. Perhaps it belonged to Mrs Mack. I wonder if I can reach it.

She stretched down into the hole. It's too deep. It's stuck, anyway. I can't get it out. It's probably not worth bothering about.

But somehow she thought Callum wouldn't have given up so easily.

'It's all right for him. He's got strong arms.'

But she picked up the trowel and clambered down into the hole.

A worm wriggled around in the freshly dug earth, but luckily Julie didn't mind worms. She started to clear some soil around the curved piece of pot.

'It's not just a small broken piece. It's a whole pot, and it's not a teapot either, because it hasn't got a spout. Oh, Callum, why aren't you here to help me see what this is.'

She stopped for a rest and looked back at the Place. I wonder if the people who built those houses buried the pot? But why would they have done that? Perhaps it wasn't them at all. Someone else may have buried it, hundreds of years ago, perhaps even a thousand years ago, when the stone cross was still standing. Or perhaps when it was broken. Yes, that might have been it. 'No, Sarna, don't get back in. Stop it! You're sending earth on top of me. Come on, I'll take you home.'

She shut Sarna up in the porch. 'I'll get you some water. . . . Yes, I thought you'd be thirsty!'

Then Julie went back to her digging.

'It must be near to coming out now.' She was getting more and more of the pot loose. And now she could see a bit more of the cloth as well. The pot had been wrapped in several layers of cloth, but most of the material had rotted away.

'So it must have been buried a long time ago,' Julie decided.

Of course, what she should have done was mark the place and write to Dr Dickson to get the area properly examined and the pot and the cloth dug out by experts. But Julie didn't know this, and she tore what was left of the cloth quite badly as she attacked the earth with her trowel and tugged at the buried pot.

And finally she yanked it free.

And. . . .

'Oh!' exclaimed Julie, rubbing her hair back from her hot forehead. 'Ohhhhh! I've found it! I've found the secret the Place was waiting to show us. And Callum isn't here to see. No one's here. Just me . . . and this treasure.'

Clutching her treasure, Julie clambered out of the hole.

'The Place . . . . I'll look at it there.'

Kneeling beside their ruined hearth Julie set the pot on the ground. Its neck was stuffed with cloth. Julie hated the feel of it. It smelt fusty and it crumbled as her fingers touched it.

I don't like this. Perhaps the pot's all full of this old cloth. Or else there'll be a skeleton inside, bones, like in the museum.

She sat back on her heels, thinking.

Mum's gardening gloves!

She set the pot carefully in the middle of the fireplace and ran to the shed. I hate wearing rubber gloves, she thought, but it's better than touching whatever's in the pot.

With the gloves safely on Julie pulled more boldly at the cloth. More and more of it came away, but still there was no sign of any treasure.

There's nothing here after all! Then, through the glove, Julie's right hand touched something hard. She pulled away the last handful of cloth and looked inside the pot.

It's like tin. Looks a bit like a box. But still she was glad of the gloves. It's not very big, a bit like a money box. Gently she eased the box out of the pot. And now she pulled off her gloves and held the box between her hands.

It's silver, I think . . . shaped like a little house. Perhaps these stones round the edges are pearls. One seems to be missing. I wonder if it's fallen off somewhere inside the pot.

She tipped the pot upside down and there amongst gravel and dust and bits of frayed cloth was a dull little pearl. Julie fitted it back in place. It needs to be stuck down properly, of course, she thought, but holding the pearl in place with one finger, Julie shook the box. It didn't rattle.

So there's no money inside.

Clouds scudded in the April sky. The cows lowed from the field below the road.

Why wasn't Callum here to share in the find? Julie felt as though she didn't want to open the box without her friend. She looked at the lid for a long time. There were more twisty patterns and four things like heads.

Animals, perhaps. No, this one's a bird, and that could be a person. . . . I wonder what's inside?

At first she couldn't open the lid at all, but then, as her fingers probed beneath the rim set with those dull pearls and curved spirals she must have released a catch of some sort. The lid opened easily.

Inside were pieces of folded parchment covered with

writing which Julie couldn't read.

She sat back on her heels.

No gold or silver. Mrs Mack was wrong after all. But the box is silver, I suppose. . . .

A car engine purred. A door slammed. Footsteps came up the drive.

'It's Dr Brown. He must have had a lift home. That means it's dinner time. I'll have to go to the farm.'

Dr Brown would know what to do. But suddenly Julie didn't want to take the little box away from the Place. She stood up and called, 'Dr Bro-wn! Coo-ee! It's Julie. Please come. I've got something to show you.'

And now she realised her legs were shaking.

'What is it, Julie? Been digging? Why, what's the matter?'

'Callum should be here.'

'He'll be back soon. You mustn't worry, dear. It's only a small operation.' But then Dr Brown noticed the pot and the silver box.

'What have you got here, Julie?'

Her words tumbled out as she held the box out to him. 'I wanted to make the Place nice . . . digging . . . but it isn't silver after all, I mean the box is, but not inside. But I'm sure it's Mrs Mack's treasure. . . . Careful, there's a stone loose.'

And now Dr Brown was holding the box between his broad fingers and was clearly as excited as Julie.

'Oh, Julie, what a beautiful thing! Yes, it's silver, and don't worry that there's no money inside. There's something else that's very precious indeed. Those are illuminated manuscripts. They're part of a handwritten Bible, do you see, with all the capital letters made into pictures.'

But Julie was more interested in the silver box. 'Do you think these stones are pearls?'

'River pearls, I should think. Julie, you've found a very great treasure indeed. We'll have to phone our friend Dr Dickson.'

'Not her again!'

'Yes, we must let her know all about it. It's a tremendous find.'

'I wish Callum were here! And, Dr Brown, why do you think the box got hidden away like that?'

'Invaders perhaps, troubled times. Who knows? Show me exactly where you found it, Julie.'

'Here, just beside the fireplace. Sarna dug a hole.'

'Let's put a stone here to mark the exact spot. There. And now you must put that precious box in a very safe place and I'll phone Dr Dickson at once.'

'And then I'll take Sarna to the farm because it's dinner time,' said Julie.

# 11

## 'It's a treasure place!'

'What a wonderful find! I'll take it right back to Glasgow and try to get it dated,' said Dr Dickson.

'But you've just driven all the way from Glasgow!' Dr Brown offered the archaeologist coffee.

'I'm used to driving. I want to get an opinion on it as soon as possible.'

'Then Julie and I have a request . . .'

'Could you call by Queen Margaret Hospital and let Callum see our treasure too?'

And after she'd thought it over, Dr Dickson agreed. 'Why don't I take Julie too?' she offered.

'But how would I get home?'

'Isn't there a bus?'

'That's very kind of you,' said Dr Brown. 'Why not phone your mother, Julie, and check it out with her?'

And so it was decided that Julie should go too. Dr Brown gave her money for her fare home.

Dr Dickson put the pot and the cloth in a polythene bag and packed them into the boot of her car, but Julie kept the silver box.

'I want to keep looking at it.'

'Fine, only please don't handle the manuscripts.'

But in fact Julie fell asleep as the car headed eastwards.

They found Callum with both legs in plaster lying on top of his bed in a sunny ward.

'Julie! Hi! What are you doing here? Hullo, Dr Dickson.'

'How was the operation?' Dr Dickson pulled a chair

beside the bed.

'Fine. My toes should be straighter now. But what's this box, Julie?'

'Treasure. Mrs Mack's treasure. Here. . . .'

'Gently, children, *please*,' moaned Dr Dickson, 'It's very precious.'

'Sarna dug a hole,' Julie poured out her story.

We should both be in the Place, she thought, with the larches and larks singing. Aloud she said, 'It's almost a thousand years old, isn't it, Dr Dickson?'

'We don't know yet, perhaps about that and the manuscripts may well be slightly older.'

'And you found it all by yourself,' said Callum.

'With Sarna, but I hoped I'd find silver.'

'You've read too many adventure stories,' Dr Dickson pushed her glasses up her nose. Julie and Callum shot looks at each other which said, 'She doesn't know about Mrs Mack.'

'The scribe who wrote those pages would seldom have seen silver,' Dr Dickson said. 'Poor folk would give him meal and corn, a loaf or an oatcake in exchange for his prayers. And the king in his fort at Dunadd would give gold coins to the Abbot or Bishop to buy paint and ink and vellum. Can you picture the smile on the face of our scribe then?'

'Yes, but who was the scribe?'

'Just a man living alone in a hut of willow or of hazel beside the burn at the foot of the hill. . . .'

'Close to the stone cross,' suggested Callum.

'With deer visiting him?' added Julie.

'It would be so still in his hut that the deer might well come nosing close. Our scribe, let's call him Brother Cormac, would paint their pictures in the letters he wrote . . . see.' Sure enough as Dr Dickson unfolded one of the precious manuscripts the children saw the picture of a brown deer in the heart of one of the letters.

Dr Dickson's much nicer now she's talking about Brother Cormac, Julie thought. She makes it feel as if we were all sitting in the Place.

And now Julie and Callum could imagine the humming of bees on an August day and barefoot children leaving Brother Cormac a present of honey in its comb.

'Thank you children,' Brother Cormac might say, smiling above his feather pen. 'You put sweetness in my mouth, and I put sweetness in your hearts, because, as the Psalm I'm writing here says, the word of the Lord is sweeter than honey.'

'And, you see, he wrote that Psalm in his manuscript,' Dr Dickson said, pointing to the curving letters on the parchment.

Julie tried to make out the Latin words. 'What's a psalm?' she asked,

'And how did the manuscript get buried?' Callum wanted to know.

'A psalm is a song to God,' Dr Dickson answered Julie's question first. 'It's hard to say about the manuscript. It would be during a dark time of war and unrest, perhaps the very time when the stone cross got broken. Someone obviously hid the parchments inside the little box and buried them. Perhaps the person hoped to come back later and find them again. But it never happened, and the cross lay broken there on the field. Years later people would take the broken bits away and build them into their fine new houses. . . . But now I must rush and catch a professor whom I know will be interested in this,' Dr Dickson finished briskly. 'Are you ready, Julie?'

'Thanks for coming in and telling me all about it,' said Callum.

'See you Saturday.' But Dr Dickson was already ushering Julie away.

Saturday brought Callum, three newspaper reporters and an outside broadcast team with cameras and equipment.

'We're going to be on the news!' said Julie. 'You must take photographs of Callum too. And Sarna.'

And they did.

Next day Callum and Julie were in six different papers, as well as on the television news. In the papers headlines said things like:

**Treasure seekers follow a dog**
**Puppy digs up buried treasure**
**Amateur archaeologists make a find.**
**'I only wanted to dig a garden for my friend'**
**Treasure trove Julie's lucky find.**

The phone rang all day Sunday with calls from people who were interested in archaeology or local history, but as the April evening sun went down, Julie pushed Callum's wheelchair through long shadows to the Place. Sarna bounded around them, then lay down beside the chair.

'Mum says she's fed up being the parent of a television star,' said Julie.

'They'll have forgotten all about us by tomorrow,' Callum told her.

'No one knows about Mrs Mack. How do you think she knew about the treasure, Callum?'

'Dad says the story must have been handed down like a piece of, what did he call it – folklore, I think, and that it got a bit muddled up as it got told!' But then Callum's hand shot out and gripped Julie's arm, 'Look, Julie. A deer.'

Beyond the Place, right at the edge of the forest a young deer bent its brown head to graze, and in the self-same moment they both noticed the creamy fleck behind the quivering ears.

'*Our* deer,' breathed Callum.

But it was hardly there before it lifted its head and bounded away.

'It survived the winter then,' said Callum.

'Perhaps it comes so close to the Place because it remembers its mother getting hay here,' reflected Julie. 'I'm glad we've seen it again.' Then Julie noticed the time on Callum's watch. 'I'll have to go,' she said, 'Dad's phoning tonight. I don't want to miss his call.'

Later that evening a phone call came from Yaristan.

'Julie, come and speak now . . . here you are.' As her mother handed over the receiver she said, 'Dad's got good news for us.'

'Hullo, Julie,' her father's voice seemed so close it was hard to think he wasn't just down the road. 'You've been having an exciting day, I hear.'

'And we've just seen our deer, the one I told you about last winter. But what's your good news?'

'Can you get some nice warm weather organised for me, Julie? I'll be home three weeks from tonight.'

'Three weeks . . . oh, that's great. Have you got a suntan?'

'Not really. It's too hot to lie around in the sun.'

'Mum wants the phone back, but just tell me quickly. Have you ever seen that girl, the one who sang the song?'

'Isha? Mum will be able to tell you all about her.'

Julie could hardly wait for her mother to come off the phone.

'Dad and I have decided that we'll try to sponsor Isha through school, and college,' her mother explained.

'You mean she'll come and live here?'

'No. We'll do it all by post. We shall write to her. She'll find someone to translate the letters. And every month we'll send money to help her and her family. Jim and Jean want to help too. Isha is good·at sewing and weaving. Dad has bought some of the things she's made. Once she's fully trained she'll be able to teach other girls in the village and help them sell their things too.'

Julie told Callum about it in the Place.

'I've always wanted a sister.' Julie said.

'So have I, or a brother,' agreed Callum.

'So we can share Isha. Just think, it all happened because Dad went to church at Easter.'

'And he went to church because of your letters.'

'And I wrote them because I was happy because we

were friends. And because of the Place.'

'Our treasure Place,' said Callum.

'I'll tell Isha all about it,' Julie said.

*Dear Isha,*

*We're almost sisters so I want to tell you about our Place.*
*It's a treasure Place because me and Callum found a stone*
*there. Sarna, that's my dog, dug a hole and I found a pot*
*with a silver box inside. There were hand-written pages*
*of the Bible inside the box. Someone hid them years ago.*
*I'm telling you all about it because your singing made Dad*
*happy.*

*Lots of love,*

*Julie.*

*P.S. Callum sends his love and so do his mum and dad.*
*Callum is my best friend, but so are you.*

Julie drew a picture of Sarna at the end of her letter and
her mother helped her to write the address.

'I'm glad we moved here, Mum, aren't you?'

'We certainly didn't know that hidden treasure lay in
store,' her mother smiled. Then with Sarna at their heels
they walked to the pillar box to post Julie's letter from
Ballonoch to Yaristan.